TOXIC

LUCY V HAY is an author and script editor for movies and short film. She was never one of the 'popular girls' at school and lived in a rural area, just like Winby in The Intersection Series. The target of 'Mean Girls' herself, Lucy decided to write a story that brought forth the complications and struggles of growing up a girl.

She lives in Devon, UK with her husband, three children, five cats and three Great African Land Snails.

LUCY V HAY

TOXIC

Littwitz
PRESS

COPYRIGHT

Littwitz Press
Dahl House, Brookside Crescent
Exeter EX4 8NE

Copyright © Lucy V Hay and Littwitz Press 2018

Lucy V Hay has asserted her rights to be identified
as the author of this work in accordance with the
Copyright, Designs and Patents Act 1988.

First published in Great Britain by Littwitz Press in 2018

www.littwitzpress.com

A CIP catalogue record for this book is available
from the British Library.

ISBN: 978-1-9993501-1-6

All rights reserved. No part of this book may be copied,
or transmitted in any form or by any means, electronic, electrostatic,
magnetic tape, mechanical, photocopying,
recording or otherwise, without the written permission of
the author Lucy V Hay and Littwitz Press.

To Lilirose and all girls who have suffered because of
Queen Bees and frenemies:
Remember, people don't do things because of YOU,
they do them because of THEMSELVES.

Stay true to yourself and do the right thing.
You will never regret it.

'You have to know what you stand for,
not just what you stand against.'
– *Laurie Halse Anderson*

Prologue

Saturday, August 25th

I opened the Snapchat message and immediately wished I hadn't. In plain, accusing black type: *YOU TELL HER OR I WILL*. A selection of emojis accompanied the message, including angry faces, pointy fingers and fists.

Ellie wanted to make sure I knew she really meant it.

I sighed and slid my phone into the back pocket of my jeans. I picked up the cup and plate from beside the till. My best friend Olivia sat at one of the little aluminium tables and chairs in the The Teddy Bear's Picnic. A tourist trap, the café was nineties chic by today's standards, though in reality the last time it had been decorated was twenty years ago. What goes around, comes around. Or so they say.

As I approached, Olivia scrolled through her phone, her expression impassive. She double-tapped on the screen as she did so, one after another. Behind her was a faded mural of various soft toys dancing and drinking from faded tea cups. Various teenagers had added to it over the years. One of the rag dolls now sported what was supposed to be a machine gun and proclaimed in a large speech bubble, '*You can't sit here.'* Ah, *Mean Girls*. Classic.

'Anything interesting online?' I wondered aloud, placing the cup and pastry in front of my best friend.

Olivia slung her phone down on the table top with a grimace. 'Oh … just some idiot making comments on my Insta.'

'Ignore them,' I replied, 'they're looking for a reaction.'

As I said this, I was ultra-aware of my mobile, crammed under my left bum cheek on the metal chair. God, I was such a hypocrite! I plucked at the frayed knees of my jeans, unable to look Olivia in the eye.

Olivia smiled. 'So, what's the plan?'

That was Olivia-speak for *What are we doing today?* I shrugged, feeling the betrayal between my shoulder blades.

'Share it with me?' Olivia smiled, pushing the mug towards me.

'I don't like hot chocolate.' I didn't allow myself to have such calorific foods when I was training.

'Everyone likes hot chocolate!' Olivia rebuffed.

She touched the top of the cream with her fingertip, licking it off daintily. She was wearing a bright neon pink vest top; a giant smiley face proclaimed on the front, FOR REAL.

Olivia's eyes narrowed. '… What's the matter?'

'Nothing.' I said automatically.

~

I'd seen Ellie that morning at the window of her parents' just-as-perfect seafront house, The Grange, as I ran across the beach. She'd spotted me too and waved me up. I'd run gladly up the steps and hopped over the sea wall, through her living room patio window. I stood next to her, sweaty, my hair tousled and matted. Ellie eyed me up and down.

'You're such a masochist.' Ellie drawled in that half-joking, half-for-real way that always kept me off-balance.

I blotted my hands on my tracky bottoms. 'Running's good for you?'

'We're seventeen, Jaz,' Ellie rolled her eyes. 'You should be having more fun!'

'I have fun.' I protested, my hackles rising. Ellie's sardonic smile irritated me, but I wasn't really sure why. I didn't care if she liked running or not. Did I?

Ellie busied herself making toast. Even first thing in the morning, straight out of bed and her hair unbrushed, it was impossible not to think of Ellie as anything other than flawless. *Little Miss Popular*, Olivia would have sneered. And Olivia was not wrong: blonde-haired, blue-eyed, Ellie was the poster girl for classic beauty. Girls wanted to be her and boys, well … just wanted her.

And Ellie knew it.

She grinned, taking a bite of toast. 'Guess what? The parentage is going away tonight. Party time!'

I spotted one problem immediately. 'What about Ste?'

'God Jaz, you're such a downer.' Ellie said, wide-eyed.

At twenty-one, Ste was the eldest of the three Mackintosh siblings and definitely the straightest. Most weekends he could be found on the first-floor balcony of their home, The Grange, which overlooked Winby seafront. His nose in a book, he'd have one eye watching the world go by underneath. It was hard to believe Ellie and her other brother Niall were related to him, though Ellie explained it by saying Ste had a different Dad. Did it make that much difference? I had no clue … I was an only child.

The Mackintoshes were in a different league anyway: I lived in a pokey, damp flat with my mum, who could only get seasonal work thirty-six weeks of the year if she was lucky. The Mackintoshes had the best of everything. Ellie was decked out in designer gear at her posh private school back in London. The Grange was just their summer home on the beachfront in our little seaside town, Winby.

'The olds actually said we could have a party if you must know.' Ellie raised her eyebrows, challenging me.

'… As long as Ste supervised?' I guessed. By the irritated look on Ellie's face, correctly.

'It'll be good.' Ellie insisted. 'I'll sort it. But look, Olivia is not invited.'

An actual physical pain stabbed me in the stomach at Ellie's words: first hurt, then anger for my best friend. Yet like a coward I just stood there. I didn't challenge Ellie. What kind of friend was I?

'Then I won't come.' I said, in a small voice. Ellie couldn't be serious. This was so juvenile. We were seventeen, not seven!

'I'm serious.' Ellie dashed my hopes. 'I'm sick of her, bringing the place down with her attitude. And mooning around Ste … It's grotesque! Anyway, you have to come, Jaz. Becky Jarvis will be there.'

Becky. My Achilles Heel. She had been sniffing around Niall since the beginning of the summer. With her long blonde hair and ice-blue eyes, she could give even Ellie a run for her money in the beauty stakes. And Ellie knew that. She was counting on me wanting to be there, just in case.

The Mackintoshes had seemed to arrive in Winby a long time before the family actually set in the town. There was a massive SOLD sign in the window of The Grange, which had stood empty for years before that. The locals had speculated for months: what would it become? Some thought it would become a hotel again, or maybe an art gallery. Most thought it would be turned into yet more tourist flats.

Then one day, just before the schools had broken up, a huge van had come. Two burly men had unloaded new, expensive furniture still wrapped in plastic. Most people assumed at first the Mackintoshes would be town-dwellers, rather than tourists, or 'grockles' as the locals liked to call them. Several Winby residents gathered on The Moon steps, a seafront pub opposite The Grange.

A well-dressed woman in her late forties or perhaps early fifties – Charlotte, Ellie and the boys' Mum - got out of an expensive car and waved to them, a wide smile on her over-pink lips and rouged cheeks.

'Hi there!' Charlotte trilled to the locals, her accent quite different to ours, cutting through the air like a foreign language. One Winby local, already holding a pint at just eleven am, raised a single hand in return.

I'd paid no attention to the movers. I didn't care whether a bunch of toffee-nosed grockles were moving in. On the beach, I burst forth across the shale and up the steps, jumping them two or three at a time. I'd run straight into Niall Mackintosh, on his way down. Calloused hands grabbed me before I could fall backwards down the steps.

'Whoa there.' Niall said, a grin as wide as the Cheshire cat's.

'Sorry.' I jerked away from his touch. Niall was tall, dark, good-looking. Thin, his skin stretched over his tall, angled skeleton too tight, covered in scratches and grazes, betraying an outdoors life: knuckles, elbows, knees.

'Don't worry about it.' Niall moved aside to let me pass.

I just stood there, like an idiot. So, in an exaggerated move, he squeezed by me to the next step, chuckling to himself. He skipped, hopped and jumped down to the shale. Left behind, I just stared after him, as if willing him to turn around. I watched him for a few seconds, then turned and ran up the rest of the steps, certain I could feel his gaze on my back.

'He sounds delish.' Olivia had declared that first day, lolling on her bed. She had a gigantic-sized packet of bacon crisps for breakfast in front of her. Past midday, she hadn't even got up yet.

'He's a poser.' I said in a sour mood, though I wasn't sure why. To distract her, I ripped the duvet off my best friend. She shrieked and bacon crisps flew up in the air.

'Right, that's it.' Olivia proclaimed, 'This means war!'

Olivia fell on me, her heavier weight knocking the breath out of me. We sprawled on the bed, grabbing and tickling each other, howling with laughter. This was the way it had always been: me and Olivia, best of friends since nursery school. On our first day I'd seen her moping in the corner on her own. I'd had a skipping rope and tried to teach her how; she'd hit me in the head with one of the plastic handles. We'd been inseparable ever since.

'Girls.' A low voice growled.

Both of us froze in an instant. Jim, Olivia's Dad stood in the doorway, black coffee in hand, that strained expression on his face. I'd not seen anything else painted on his features since Olivia's Mum, Polly, had left two years' previously. Perhaps that was because he always had a permanent hangover, too. The cupboards might well have been Mother Hubbard's when it came to food, but there wasn't a single shelf in the house without a half-empty bottle of booze on it.

'What would you like for dinner?' Olivia would say airily, 'Harvey Wallbanger? Sex On The Beach? LIGHTER FLUID?'

Jim would just snarl and throw a selection of change down on the kitchen table. Olivia became the best patron of The Penguin Fish Bar down on the seafront. Their battered sausages were ace, even for a fit-freak like me. But I still tried to persuade Olivia to have her dinner with me and Mum at least once a week.

'Sorry Dad,' Olivia said, clearly not meaning it as she slammed the door in his face. 'So! What's the plan?'

'The plan?' I was genuinely bewildered.

'For today.' Olivia said. She groaned. 'You know your problem Jasmine? You have no aspirations.'

'As if.' I tutted.

I had plans, though all centred around getting into university. I'd gone to the college careers fair, dragging Olivia after me. As she chatted up soldiers and tradesmen looking for new recruits and apprentices, I had approached every single academic institution. I'd grilled them about tuition fees, league table rankings and their graduates' earnings. I'd left with a huge bagful of prospectuses, bumper stickers and fluffy stick-on mascots. I dragged it all home with me and told Mum about it.

'It's up to you, darling.' Mum barely looked up from the television.

I'd felt oddly betrayed. Didn't she want me to do well? Wasn't she proud her only child was a good student?

'I thought you'd be pleased.' I said quietly.

'Of course I am.' Mum said, meeting my eye at last with a wide smile. 'But it's your life, Jaz. I don't want to influence you. You must do what you want.'

This is what I never got with my Mum. She was an advocate of what she called 'hands off parenting'. In comparison to most of the parenting articles I read online – yes, I read parenting articles, in a bid to get where she was coming from – Mum seemed to believe teenagers needed to make their own mistakes and learn from them that way. Personally, I would rather make no mistakes at all. Wasn't she supposed to help me avoid them?

'It doesn't matter what I say,' Mum explained, 'You'll do what you want anyway. What's the point of creating conflict for the sake of it? Just know that I'm here if you need me.'

But are you? I wanted to say. But didn't. As always. Uncertainty seemed to rule my life. I couldn't trust myself to make the right decision, not without guidance. I'd never done all this life stuff before. I tried to say this to Mum, but she was having none of it.

'You've got to have faith in yourself.' She said, as if that made it all better.

Mum was a hypocrite, anyway. Her life had hardly been easy. With no qualifications and little experience, Mum picked up work where she could in Winby and Exmorton. At the moment she worked at Flossie's, a beach shop sandwiched between The Penguin Fish Bar and The Moon pub, selling seaside rock, fluorescent flip flops, buckets and spades, magnets and postcards and other tourist dross.

In Olivia's bedroom, my best friend checked some rumpled clothes for the smell of smoke, wrinkling her nose in distaste.

'These all whiff!' She exclaimed. 'And in fact, so do you athlete girl. Go home, get showered, meet me on the seafront in half an hour.'

'What for?' I grumbled.

'What do you think?' Olivia grinned.

I found myself back on the seafront with Olivia as instructed, pretending not to look like we were spying on The Mackintoshes as they continued to move in. Or rather, as the removal people moved them in. Charlotte, Tom and Ste sat on the first-floor balcony watching, a jug of iced tea between them. I craned my neck to see if Niall sat with them and feigned nonchalance when Olivia caught my eye.

'Lover boy not there?' There was a devilish twinkle in her eye I knew too well.

'Oh … No. Don't. Don't do it … !' I began.

Too late. Olivia waved up to the Mackintoshes. Charlotte waved back, beaming. With skilful ease, Olivia ingratiated herself with the older woman, complimenting her on her outfit and the house. Before five minutes were gone, Olivia and I had been invited up. I was forced to follow Olivia up to the balcony. We were pulling our chairs in at record speed, even for Olivia, such was Charlotte's desire to meet and converse with the locals.

'This is Steven, my eldest.' Charlotte said proudly.

Blonde, his top collar button done up, Ste cut a strange figure next to his parents. But under his nerdish attire – a cable-knit sweater, seriously? – it was plain to see Ste was as good-looking as Niall, albeit in a different way. Olivia had certainly noticed, glancing at him sideways every time she had the chance. Not that Ste had any clue, his nose was buried in a book.

'I believe you've met my other son, Niall?' Charlotte fixed me in her sights. 'It was you I saw on the beach, running?'

'Yes.' I muttered, self-conscious.

Charlotte smiled again. She had huge, white teeth. 'So good to see young people with a hobby! Do you run for the county, dear?'

'No, not yet.' I said, lack-lustre. For some crazy reason I felt like I wanted to please her. 'But I plan to do sports science at university next year?'

'How wonderful!' Charlotte said. 'Isn't that wonderful, Tom?'

Her quiet, grey-haired husband nodded, all the while looking out to sea. As Charlotte turned to look at him in irritation, Olivia pulled a face at me. I had to bite my cheek to stop from laughing. In a rare moment looking up from his book, Ste regarded us in bewilderment.

'So, girls,' Charlotte said breezily, bidding Tom to fetch more glasses with a simple flick of her hand, 'What are your names?'

'I'm Olivia and this is Jasmine.' Olivia took a huge slurp of iced tea.

'Jasmine! One of my absolute favourite scents. Isn't that right, Tom? I wore a jasmine perfume on our wedding day.' Tom nodded almost imperceptibly. Charlotte remembered herself: 'And Olivia... Well. If I hadn't chosen Ellie for my daughter, that was my second choice ... Darling, there you are!'

On cue, Ellie arrived at the open patio window. Our age and dressed in a simple red sundress with red flip flops, this was a girl who took accessorising to the max. There was a red flower in her hair, red frame sunglasses, even a red beaded bag over her shoulder. And she knew she looked fantastic.

'This place is totally dead.' Ellie confirmed. She looked over the bridge of her sunglasses at me and Olivia. ' ... Oh.

Hello.'

'Hi,' I felt like I'd only pulled on a sack that morning, yet I had to admit to taking extra care getting ready in case Niall was there. I'd even put on make-up.

'Have some tapas darling, you're all skin and bones.' Charlotte commanded.

On the expensive patio set table was deep earthenware dish of olives, peppers, hummus and a selection of dips. These were all things that were strictly treats in my house; Mum's budget didn't stretch to fancy snacks on an ordinary day. Charlotte must have seen my wide eyes because she offered me the over-sized platter. Mortified, I pretended I wasn't hungry, even though in reality I was ravenous. I prayed my stomach would not rumble and give me away.

Ellie picked up a single olive, popping it in her mouth. Her father immediately brought Ellie a chair. She sat down without thanking him, or even seeming to notice him. Invisible man.

'Hi, I'm Olivia.' Olivia repeated, extending a hand towards Ellie. She was positively drinking Ellie and her sophisticated cool in.

Ellie looked at Olivia's hand a moment: her chipped nail varnish, the collection of rings on her chubby fingers, the homemade bobbles and bracelets on her wrist. Ellie smiled politely and gave it a limp shake.

'So, do you expect Niall back anytime soon?' Olivia said.

I shot daggers at her, but my best friend paid no attention.

'He can't have got far.' Ellie yawned. 'This place is the size of a cat basket.'

'I'm sure there's lots of fun things to do in Winby,' Charlotte mock-scolded her daughter. 'Olivia and Jasmine would be glad to show you, I'm sure?'

Olivia picked up on the invitation in an instant, her best behaviour returned. 'Yes, of course! We'd be happy to. How about tomorrow?'

Ellie's smile froze. 'I think I'm busy tomorrow.'

'Doing what, Sis?' Ste enquired, a sardonic look on his face.

'Unpacking.' Ellie replied, deadpan.

'Oh, that won't take all day!' Charlotte proclaimed. 'Well that's settled, then. How about ten tomorrow, girls? You can show Ellie the sights!'

As promised, we did. Or rather, we dragged Ellie around, showing her Winby's seafront gardens; the crazy golf putting green; the helter-skelter and children's play park. Later in the week, Ellie was as underwhelmed by Exmorton too, complaining even the chain stores were small and poky in comparison to 'back home'. Olivia's interest in Ellie quickly palled.

'Stuck up cow.' Olivia whispered to me as Ellie wandered off, scrolling through her phone.

I found myself defending the new girl for some reason. 'It's all just new to her.'

'She thinks she's better than us.' Olivia folded her arms. 'Actually, no. She thinks she's better than me.'

Dismay flooded through me. I wanted them to get on. 'I'm sure that's not true.'

That Friday night, Ellie did seem to perk up when she saw the local boys gathering down on Winby Cove.

'Who are they?' She asked, her eyes darting over every last one of them.

Down on the shale, Andrew Franklin and friends laughed

and joked, hopping over the river that lead out to the cove. We'd gone to school with Andrew; he was in my A Level Biology class at college now. He was harmless, even a good laugh from time to time.

'I'll introduce you.' I said to Ellie, ignoring the look I got from Olivia.

We went down to speak to the boys, Ellie all starry-eyed and Olivia hanging back, scowling. The lads laughed and bantered about our lack of ability to make it over the river on our own. Andrew even helped Ellie jump over, holding her hand.

Back at Ellie's, in-between bottles of cheap cider, Ellie told both of us all about her life in London. The shops. The clubs. The guys. It sounded totally amazing. I told Ellie I wanted to study in the Capital.

'You don't study in London!' Ellie laughed, making me feel off-balance again. 'You live the *lifestyle*.'

'What's that supposed to mean?' Olivia demanded, yet another sour expression on her face.

It was a look I was getting used to seeing more and more every day. *Lighten up*, I wanted to say, yet felt I couldn't. She was my best friend, after all. As the weeks went on, the chasm between Ellie and Olivia continued to widen.

'She said my dress was 'interesting'.' Olivia complained, looking at herself sideways in the mirror. She was wearing a purple halterneck dress, more than a little too short and too small at the arms. Her chubby back spilled over the top, pinching at her greying bra straps.

'That doesn't mean she doesn't like it.' I attempted.

'Well what does it mean to Little Miss Popular, then?' Olivia challenged, her grey eyes flashing. 'You're best friends now, you tell me.'

I'd heard this all before. 'We're not best friends,' I said, slowly and patiently, as if talking to a five-year-old. '*You*'re my best friend.'

'Oh really? Could've fooled me.' Olivia accused, her lip quivering.

'What's that supposed to mean!' I snapped.

But deep down, a small part of me knew Olivia was right. I didn't stand up for her like I might have done at school when Colin Knowles dunked the ends of Olivia's unruly plaits in the PVA glue that time art class; or the time David Hunt tripped her over walking out of science. But this was different. Ellie wasn't doing anything specific, other than being, well ... Just *Ellie*. She was the same with everyone: that sardonic grin, the mock-raised eyebrow, that way of making you feel off-kilter, whatever you said or did. It was just the way she was.

As the summer continued, Olivia and Ellie started to compete for my attention. Messages would arrive, inviting me on my own to the shops, the seafront, their houses. I felt pulled between them. Yet still I hoped my two friends would somehow make peace and like each other as much as I liked them individually. Olivia was warm-hearted, fun and someone I could rely on in a crisis. Ellie was exotic, sophisticated, bringing with her stories of places I'd only ever seen on television. I should have known there would be a day when I would have to make a choice.

Today.

'Come on, Jaz.' At The Grange, Ellie's expression had softened, 'It's just one party. And Olivia can't stand me anyway. She called me a 'bush pig' last time she saw me – whatever the hell that is. She won't even care!'

There was a certain logic to Ellie's words. I imagined

telling Olivia about the party and her saying she wouldn't go, 'out of principle' – her latest phrase.

'Okay, fine. 'I said at last. 'But *I*'ll tell her.'

~

At Teddy's, I stared miserably into my green tea. I couldn't let my best friend down, but I couldn't *not* go to the party either. I couldn't let Becky have a free pass at Niall, my own boyfriend. I had to be there just in case. Also, if I was honest with myself, didn't I crave for a slice of what the Ellies and Beckys of this world had? I wanted to be popular too, for once. Olivia was happy being an individual, but I was tired of being marked as uncool. Why couldn't I have just this one night?

I knew it was wrong doing Ellie's dirty work for her, but I also knew Ellie would deliver the news even more devastatingly. I was doing the kindest thing … *Wasn't I?* Olivia would understand. Eventually. Besides, it would sound better coming from me than Ellie …

… *Wouldn't it?*

I take a deep breath. "Olivia, I need to tell you something …'

Block

'True friends stab you in the front.'
– *Oscar Wilde*

One

Saturday, August 25th

... The bell above Teddy's front door tinkled, as it always did when someone walks in. I blinked. The world came in on for me a second, bolder and brighter than it had before. Neon price stars, blue-tacked to the back wall behind the café counter loomed at me, advertising their misspelled and grammatically incorrect items: 'carramel wafers', 'hot chocalate', 'crisp's' and 'snack's'.

I turned to see Jenny Keller appear through the door of Teddy's. She was an art student, about to go into the second year of college this September, like me and Olivia. Jenny was juggling a couple of folders. She thought she was the 'Bohemian' type, wearing a dress over her jeans, plus endless loops of plastic beads around her neck. Was that an actual bindi on her forehead?

'Jaz … hello??' Olivia waved a hand in front of me. 'Lost you there, space cadet.'

My best friend's laugh seemed to echo in my ears. I felt disorientated, as if I had been planted there, in the café, by a giant. But that was ridiculous. *What was it I was saying?* I couldn't remember for a second.

Then it came flooding back: oh right, Ellie's party.

'Hey.' Jenny interrupted, catching our eyes as she grabbed her purse. She was also the neverendingly cheerful type, ready with a smile and a 'Hello'. We had never been friends, even at primary school. It made me feel bad hating her the way I did, so I hated her even more.

Olivia gave Jenny a polite smile back, her attention diverted by a call on her mobile. She indicated to me she needed to take it, placing the handset to her ear before I could argue.

'Yes Dad, I'm coming now.' She rolled her eyes at me, as if to say *Parents! What can you do?*

She swooped on me, kissed me on the cheek. ''Bye!'

I watched, frustrated, as my best friend stood up and moved towards the café door. The little bell rang again as she crossed the threshold. I watched Olivia disappear back up the high street, towards her house. *Blocked.* Typical.

'Looking forward to going back to college?' Jenny appeared next to me, an oversized mug of tea in hand. She fell into the chair Olivia had just vacated, uninvited.

I swallowed down my irritation. Jenny came from a long line of weirdos. Her Dad was a teacher and had taught us Geography at Winby High until her parents got a divorce. Mr. Keller became increasingly eccentric – read 'weird' - until he was 'asked' to leave. Some said he had a nervous breakdown, live in class and had threatened to chuck Jack Thompson out a window.

'Yeah, I suppose.'

Behind me, a Goth Girl about a year older than me and her Uber-Geek boyfriend talked in muted tones. I recognised her from somewhere, but I wasn't sure where. A tinny radio played muzak on a loop.

'What's that?' Jenny peered into my cup.

'Green tea.'

'Eurgh.' Jenny declared, 'That's like, so middle-aged. Why don't you have something nice, like a hot chocolate?'

'I don't like hot chocolate.'

The words felt strange in my mouth. I felt like I had said them before. I was sure I was a puppet in a theatre again, my strings attached to an over-sized child's fingers. I had a flashback to English class in Year Nine. Our teacher, Mrs Jenkin had read from Shakespeare's Merchant of Venice: *'All the world's a stage where every man must play a part. And mine a sad one.'*

'What. The. Hell.' Jenny said, 'Everyone likes hot chocolate!'

I checked my phone screen for the time: past midday. Through Teddy's window and its greying net curtains, August looked like October. It was grey, cold and raining. Mum arrived outside Flossie's opposite as puddles started filling outside the shop. British Summertime at its best. She pulled in the display board, the buckets and spades, flip flops and swimsuits. Yet still the feeling of déjà vu plagued me, giving me itchy feet.

'I have to go.' I rose from the table.

Jenny seemed untroubled. 'Suit yourself.'

That bell tinkled as I opened the café door. I stopped. There was one way I could let Olivia know about the party, yet not get the blame from Ellie: tell Jenny.

'Oh, by the way, there's a party tonight.' I threw over my shoulder as I left, '… Eight o' clock At The Grange!'

Two

I dodged Flossie's as Mum looked the other way, ducking down a side alley. She would only have a million errands for me. As per.

My phone rang as I went. A cursory look at the screen revealed it was Olivia. She probably wanted me to come up to hers. I waited a couple of rings and then cut it off, letting the call go to voicemail as I walked. I was keen to dodge Olivia. Now I thought about it, it was just easier. With a bit of luck, Olivia would see Jenny, who would drop Ellie in it. I knew I should be showing solidarity with Olivia, rather than avoiding her, but I just couldn't face the hassle. Olivia didn't like Ellie; Ellie didn't like Olivia. Why should I have to play piggy in the middle? I hadn't asked for this.

I let myself back into the flat and went straight through to my room at the back. My phone rang. Olivia again. I was careful to let it ring before cutting it off. Olivia knew I never turned my phone off. I put it on silent even in the middle of lectures at college. If I cut it off straight away, she would know something was up. When Olivia rang a third time, guilt was really beginning to kick in. I almost answered, but I forced myself to cut her off. As I knew she would, Olivia finally left a message. I listened to it as soon as she left it:

'Hi Jaz … I guess you're out. Or running. Or something.' Olivia said with forced cheeriness. I could almost hear the cogs of her brain working overtime, wondering where I was. 'Just … Give me a call when you get this, yeah?'

I sat in my room for a moment in silence. Guilt made me hyper-aware of Olivia's presence all over my room. Photos on my dressing table mirror; one of her hoodies draped on the back of the chair at my desk; on the desk, three of her textbooks she'd left behind after our last study session. Well, I say 'study session'. In reality, I was the only one who'd done any actual studying. Olivia had flipped through channels on the TV giving a derisive yet hilarious on-the-nose commentary on every Australian soap opera she could find in a fake Aussie accent.

'Oh Bruce! I had a secret affair you didn't know about twenty years ago and now my lovechild is about to knock on the door! Don't hate me!' She'd shrieked before I'd finally given up trying to study and dissolved into hysterics.

After that, we'd got dressed up and gone to the Moon Karaoke Night where we'd done a rendition of 'Valerie' to rapturous applause from the lot from the confectionary factory in Exmorton. Not long after that (it got hazy, to be honest), Mad Norman, the Moon's enormous, towering landlord had thrown us out. We'd been adding the vodka we'd hidden in our bags to our lemonades. Olivia had fallen off the high heels she'd just bought that week from the internet and broken one, so had sworn revenge. So far, she was still cooking it up.

'Revenge is a dish best served cold.' She'd declared.

I rolled my eyes. 'You have no idea what you're going to do, have you.'

'Is it that obvious?' Olivia grinned. 'Well, Norman better

watch out. I'll put a curse on him or something.' She indicated the leather-bound volume of witchcraft she'd got out the library that week.

'I bet he's shaking in his boots.' I laughed.

Back in my room, I grabbed Olivia's hoody from my chair and shoved it in the washing basket. I cleared the books off my desk, into the drawers underneath. Still Olivia's smiling face stared accusingly at me from the dressing table mirror. I took the photos off, placing them in my jewellery box, shutting the lid. *There.*

Olivia didn't even like Ellie anyway. I was entitled to go to the party without Olivia. We weren't joined at the hip like some believed. And what Olivia didn't know wouldn't hurt her; it wasn't as if I had said I wasn't going and lied to her face.

So why did I feel so bad?

I opened the jewellery box again, looking at the first photo on top of the others. In it, we were sitting on the sea wall, tinsel wound around woolly hats, next to the Christmas tree they always put up on the seafront. The Grange was still empty and boarded up behind us back then. We were about eleven; I think it was the first Christmas we'd started secondary school.

I remembered the photo being taken. Mum had insisted she and I had taken a walk on the cove beach before Christmas dinner. I hadn't wanted to go. Christmas was usually the only day of the year Mum never hassled me to get out of my pyjamas. The flat was warm, there was a film on television I wanted to watch and I had chocolate I wanted to eat. But we'd had 'words' and moments later, I was pulling on my jeans and muttering how unfair she was.

Predictably, down on the seafront the weather was harsh.

Even through a coat and two jumpers I was shivering, furious with Mum for dragging me out in such foul weather. But down on the beach was a single figure, no coat, just a woolly hat, jumper and jeans, throwing pebbles into the approaching tide: Olivia.

I looked to Mum, who smiled. I knew instantly she must have seen Olivia traipse past the house on her way to the beach. Mum nodded at me, so I went over to my best friend. Olivia's eyes were red and puffy from crying. I didn't need to ask why. Her Mum was still at home back then. Her parents had been arguing, even on Christmas Day.

'Happy Christmas.' I said at last.

Olivia regarded me, doleful. 'You're half right. It's Christmas, at least.'

'What was it about this time?'

I had seen Olivia's parents get into it scores of times before. They didn't seem to care about arguing in front of their daughters' friends, other parents at school events or even in front of strangers in the middle of the street. Nothing shamed them. I'd never forget one time when we were about nine. Olivia's younger sister, Natalie was barely out of nappies. Polly and Jim had taken us all out, supposedly for ice cream. Instead, they'd got into an argument in the middle of Spring Lanes, Exmorton's only shopping mall. The scene had lasted a full forty-five minutes and attracted a small crowd of teens outside Millie's, the ice cream parlour. We'd never even made it inside.

Olivia and I had had to stand by dumbly, dying of embarrassment. We had been unable to pry the pushchair handles out of Jim's oversized hands. Olivia hadn't wanted to leave her crying little sister with her furious parents, trading insults. Eventually Polly had grabbed us kids and stalked off to the car, leaving Jim in the middle of Exmorton. He'd found a cab home, but it hadn't even been over then. The argument had continued late into the night, Olivia said. That was a relatively short one; some of Jim and Polly's arguments could last days. Worse than that was the bad feeling that could go on for weeks or even months afterwards. It was like poison gas, hanging over everything. It was no wonder Olivia spent as much time as she could out of the house back then.

But on the beach, my best friend did not give me all the details. She didn't act out what they'd yelled at each other, ridiculing them both as she would with those Aussie soap operas. Instead, Olivia just shrugged.

'It's Christmas,' she said. 'Can't they get along for just one day?'

I didn't know what to say. I'd never lived with my Dad and my Mum had only ever had one serious boyfriend, Kevin. I'd never really known what he did for a living and I hadn't cared: something with insurance, only he was the boss.

I hugged Olivia.

We'd watched a dog chase after a new ball into the incoming tide from the sea wall: it was an exuberant golden retriever, his jaw hanging open in what looked like a wide smile. Then Mum had taken the photo of us with her phone.

'Best friends.' She'd said.

Olivia and I draped our arms around each other and posed for the camera for several photos. Yet the one I held in my hand now was a different one: a natural pose that Mum had sneaked in without us realising. Olivia was looking out to sea; I was looking up at her, a kind of adoring look on my face, as if she was the only person in the world to me right then. Perhaps she was.

When had that changed?

But I shut this thought down. Olivia was a hypocrite. All she had to do was get on with Ellie for one summer, then I wouldn't be in this position. Besides, I *needed* to go to the party, to make sure Becky Jarvis wouldn't try it on with Niall.

Olivia had to wait.

Three

If I was going to a party, I need an outfit. *Dress code: Fabulous*, Ellie had instructed.

'What's that?' I'd said awkwardly.

'You know. No jeans. But not smart casual. Better than that.' Ellie flipped her hair in that way of hers. 'And not that blue shirt you always wear. God.'

'I like my blue shirt.'

'Yeah. For the house. This is an event!' Ellie replied. 'I'm only saying this for your own good, Jaz. God. Don't be dreary!'

I pulled everything I owned out of the wardrobe and flung it down on the bed. I looked at my clothes, dejected. All of them had been bought at charity shops, in the sale or discount stores. So not 'Ellie'. All her clothes were designer labels. She'd never touched a clearance rail in her life.

Ellie had packed me off with this advice and a bunch of her magazines. Flipping through them, I checked out the spreads of celebrities in various poses. Headlines blazed: FASHION VICTIM OR FASHION ICON? I couldn't tell why some were icons or victims. Apparently, it was something to do with being 'on trend (or not)' with their colours and styles. But I thought they all looked nice enough. I guessed I couldn't be 'on trend' at all? Sigh.

I appeared out of my room. Mum was home from work and sprawled on the sofa in the living area. She did not look up, or argue as I went into her room and opened her wardrobe. Mum didn't have many going out clothes – she barely went out, she was always working – but she did have a couple of outfits reserved for weddings and other special occasions. They were at the back of the wardrobe, in dress covers, a couple of mothballs tossed in as well. I wrinkled my nose and unzipped them.

First up, a flowery twin set and coordinating skirt. No way. It was far too old even for my Mum, one of her few wardrobe errors. I remembered Mum wearing it for my Uncle Tim's wedding. He wasn't really my uncle, but my Mum's best friend Kelly's brother. It was so long ago, Tim had since divorced. His short-lived marriage had been the talk of Winby for all of five minutes. What was her name? Marion? Mary? Whatever. All I could remember was a rotund bride who cried the whole day. I'd thought it was because she was so happy she was getting married. But maybe not.

The second one was a burnt orange maxi dress. Mum had worn it to my graduation from Winby High, along with a straw boater hat and brown sunglasses and espadrilles. She'd looked fantastic. The orange had complimented her sallow skin, which as ever was perfect. I don't think Mum had ever had to worry about spots in her entire life. I knew without even trying it on that the orange dress would not suit me. I was not a dark-skinned brunette like my mother, but a pasty, strawberry blonde almost light ginger. If I wore orange I might as well have worn a sign around my neck reading: SUPER CLASH.

Which left the last dress. It was a short black dress with no sleeves, the hem ending just above the knee. Mum had last worn it to dinner with her last boyfriend, Kevin, the night she'd ended it between them. I'd liked Kevin a lot. He would read to me, every weekend he came over. Over the five years he dated Mum, we soon ran out of modern children's books, so he started to bring classic stories: *Moby Dick, Pride And Prejudice, Great Expectations*. My favourites were *Alice's Adventures In Wonderland* and its sequel, *Alice Through The Looking Glass*. Kevin conjured up different voices and accents for the characters. As well as 1950s clipped English, Alice would sometimes be Irish, Liverpudlian, Geordie – and once memorably, a Texan – but for some reason, The White Rabbit was always Scottish:

"And Alice said, "How long is forever?" Kevin read aloud one night, for the fiftieth time. Alice that evening sounded as if she was on the BBC Radio 4 shipping forecast. Abruptly, Kevin slipped into his Scottish brogue: "The White Rabbit replied, "Sometimes just one second.""

I discovered those six years flashed by in a second and suddenly, Kevin was out of our lives. I blamed Mum. I still did, if I was honest. He'd wanted to get married, be a proper family. I never really understood why Mum couldn't let Kevin be part of our lives, for real. He'd wanted to be! But then, I had never really understood Mum, full stop.

'Want to borrow it?'

I jumped. Mum was standing in the doorway, smiling at me.

'Can I?'

''Course. Keep it if you want. I won't …' Mum trailed off. We both knew what she was going to say: *I won't wear it again.*

I pecked Mum on the cheek and took the black dress back to my room. It smelled of mothballs, so I gave it a liberal spray of body spray. Better. I pulled off my clothes and slipped the dress over my head. I was not tall like Mum, so the dress came past my knees, mid-calf, but still looked good. I had smaller boobs too, so it gaped a little at the arms. I opened my jewellery box again, ignoring the pictures of Olivia. I flicked through its contents until I found what I wanted: safety pins. I tucked the gaping bits on the inside, pinning them under the armpit.

I paired the dress with my red boots, which made for a startling contrast. I grabbed a red shrug off the floor and smoothed the worst of the creases out, putting it on. I put some makeup on, including red lipstick and slid a red butterfly hairclip in my hair. Perfect. *Dress code: Fabulous*, just like Ellie instructed.

I went out into the kitchen area and did a twirl for Mum. She gave me a kiss on the cheek and made a seemingly off the cuff reference to *Not Going Too Far.* I nodded and pretended to listen, tuning back in to hear I could stay out until one, a whole hour more than usual. I whooped and gave Mum a hug.

'Make sure one of the boys walks you back from The Grange.' Mum said. 'And no funny business!'

She winked at me. Actually winked. Grim.

''Course not.' I said, not meaning it, probably because I wasn't sure what I should or shouldn't be getting up to, even at seventeen. That was even more annoying than Mum pretending she was 'down with the kids'. *Why was I such a saddo?*

As I left the flat, my phone rang again. I knew without looking it was Olivia. I looked out towards town: the seafront at the bottom of the hill, the sun was disappearing behind the horizon in a shocking red and purple sunset. If I didn't answer now, Olivia was bound to turn up at the flat. Then Mum might tell her where I was. I couldn't risk it.

'Hello?'

'Jaz.' Olivia's voice wary. 'I've been trying to get hold of you for ages.'

'Yeah, sorry. I've been in the library.' I wondered how lying came so easily to me. My Mum was always one hundred per cent truthful, even when it got her in trouble. Maybe dishonesty was in my blood from my Dad's side?

'Okay.' Olivia replied. 'Why don't you come over now? I've got vodka.'

For a second, I actually thought about turning around and walking back up the high street to Olivia's. It would be so much easier. I was dreading entering The Grange and seeing all the people from college without her. Olivia was sociable, easy to be with. I could hide in her shadow; without her, I would be exposed.

But then that new voice cut in: *if you want to be popular like Ellie, you have to go it alone. Stand on your own two feet. Prove you can do it.*

It wasn't my fault Olivia wasn't invited, I reminded myself. They were the ones who refused to get on, they were just as bad as each other. I had tried to bring the two of them together.

I took a deep breath. 'I just want to get an early night, I've got training in the morning.'

This was true, at least. There were county selection meetings coming up at the Winby Harriers Juniors club. I'd missed out by just a few seconds the year before and I'd vowed to make it this year. We were meeting up on the old

Winby road at eight o' clock in the morning.

'Oh.'

I felt a pang of guilt pierce my chest. Olivia was my best friend, what was I doing? Before I could change my mind however, Olivia was ringing off.

'See you, then.'

I put my phone back in my bag and banished guilty thoughts.

I had a party to go to.

Four

I heard the noise from The Grange before I saw it. A booming bass line emanated from the grand house, its French windows open to the cove. Teens were draped on the patio and the sea wall, even spilling out into the cove itself. Ellie had not been joking when she'd said she'd invited everyone in Winby (bar Olivia). It looked as if half of Exmorton were there too. She'd put it on WhatsApp and her Instagram story.

'What if you get overrun?' I'd fretted.

'Good.' Ellie said with the authority of someone who'd never had to face the consequences in her entire life.

I approached with dread, not recognising any of the faces on the patio. People looked to one other and then at me, smirks on their faces. Too late, I realised I was hopelessly overdressed. Teens were in tee shirts and vest tops, jeans and everyday skirts. I looked as if I was about to go to the prom. Embarrassment flooded through me. I felt my cheeks burn under the layers of makeup I'd applied.

'Jasmine!' Ellie was in front of me all of a sudden, holding a huge jug of something purple, ice cubes floating in it. She was wearing flip-flops, a flared surf-style skirt and a vest top with a rainbow on it. Her make-up, perfect as ever, was natural. 'What the hell are you wearing?'

'Dress code: Fabulous, you said.' I hissed through clenched teeth.

'Yes, last *week*.' Ellie said, with those rolled eyes of hers. 'Now it's 'On The Beach'. Didn't you check my Insta since then?'

A painfully thin girl in a surfy dress with gigantic flowers approached. She took one look at me and raised one mocking eyebrow.

She looked me up and down. 'Oh dear.'

'Vic's my friend from London. Vic, this is Jasmine.' Ellie shouted above the music, shaking her head slightly.

'Oh, so *you*'re Jasmine.' Vic said, in such a way I wasn't sure if it was a good thing or not. Suddenly I wished I had never bothered coming to the party. What the hell was I doing here?

'Go with Vic, get yourself sorted out.' Ellie's tone made it clear I didn't have a choice in the matter. Then she disappeared into a throng of teens out on the patio, flipping her hair as she went.

The bored-looking Vic made a hand gesture to follow her. I traipsed after her and into the house, dodging people as we went. There were teens everywhere: sitting on the stairs, the piano, the backs of sofas. Every available seating space was taken. More teens congregated in small groups like penguins, blocking every gangway, forcing us to squeeze past as we went from room to room.

'Jaz!' From nowhere, Niall appeared, that lopsided grin on his face. He grabbed me round the waist. 'Been waiting for you all evening. Where you been?'

'Oh, you know.' Embarrassment made me untangle myself from him. I stood back, creating space between us.

Niall seemed irritated by this. 'Anyone would think you've been avoiding me?'

'I haven't been avoiding you,' I knew how standoffish I must look, but next to me was the impatient Vic, her bony arms folded. 'Look … I have to go, all right?'

Niall shook his head and blew out his cheeks, exasperated. 'Fine.'

'I'll be back in a minute …?' I began.

'Whatever.' Niall said, turning his back on me.

I almost went after him. Instead I looked to Vic, but she'd started off again through the crowd. I tried to keep up and not lose sight of her. I had no idea where she was going in this huge house. Vic picked her way round people lolling on the stairs. I followed suit, almost standing on hands and feet, half-hearted protests from drunk teens coming after me.

At the top of the stairs I saw Vic disappear into one of The Grange's massive bathrooms. I went in: there was a free-standing bath and shower cubicle; the white tiles shone brilliantly. I could fit two of my bedroom in here.

'Right, let's get you sorted out.'

She opened a cupboard. In it, an entire pharmacy, plus a selection of make-up, cotton wool pads, toner, make-up remover, tampons and everything else a girl could need. She grabbed the makeup remover and a cotton wool ball, dabbing it on my face before I could object. Downstairs, the pumping bassline continued as another song kicked in.

'Red lipstick.' Vic tutted, 'What were you thinking?'

'It went with my boots.' I said, miserable.

'This season is all about the natural look.' Vic said, as if I was an imbecile.

Who cares, a rebellious voice in my head said. But I listened, mute, as Vic finished taking off my heavy makeup, all the while telling me about accessorising and the importance of being On Trend. She opened another cupboard: inside was a washing hanger and a selection of Ellie's tee shirts and skirts. She pulled a bright pink tee shirt out with the slogan on it, THE GAME (YOU JUST LOST) and presented it to me. I hesitated. I never wore shirts like that.

'Put it on over your dress.' Vic instructed. 'None of Ellie's skirts will fit you. She's too tiny.'

I sighed. Only Ellie and her friends could make me, a size ten, feel the size of a whale. The tee shirt was still slightly damp and smelt musty, but I pulled it over my head. Now my dress just looked like a black skirt. My red boots clashed, so I took them off. Other teens downstairs were in bare feet, kicking off flip flops and sandals.

Vic grabbed some make-up from the first cupboard and applied some light foundation, powder and a touch of pink lipstick, the same shade as the tee shirt. I looked in the mirror and smiled. I looked good.

'That'll have to do.' Vic declared.

Thanks a lot. I felt like crap all over again. Before I could say anything, the bass line downstairs stopped abruptly.

'Uh oh.' Vic said, 'Now what?'

Five

We appeared out of the bathroom. Bleary-eyed teens were wandering about in a daze in the corridor, unsure of what had happened either. The lull in the music made me take in the drunk faces around me. I knew I'd blown it with Niall, regardless of Becky Jarvis. Our relationship had never got off the ground, not really. I'd spent the whole summer trying to get to know his little sister, rather than him. What the hell was I doing? I needed to get out of here.

'Are the police here?' Vic demanded of a boy in a tee shirt with a Superman logo at the top of the stairs.

I saw it was Andrew Franklin. His eyes on the verge of closing, he shrugged. Jenny Keller leaned against him, an unlit cigarette between her fingers as she attempted to light it with a Zippo, the wheel going round and round, no spark. The music came back on to a cluster of cheers downstairs.

'False alarm.' Vic said.

Carrying my red boots, I tried to squeeze past, but Jenny grabbed my skirt hem, pulling me back a second.

'I saw Olivia.' Jenny slurred.

'Did you tell her about the party?' I said with trepidation.

''Course.' Jenny smiled, but my face must have given it away, because her smile vanished just as quick. ' … Was I not meant to?'

Was I not meant to. Of course Jenny was supposed to tell Olivia. That was why I had told Jenny in the first place! But I had expected Olivia to breeze into the party. So far she hadn't shown. I was out of my depth, alone, no friends. Niall was annoyed with me. It didn't seem worth it anymore.

'Jaz!' Ellie materialised next to me, presenting me with a cocktail, complete with umbrella. 'Here you go, it's like, two thirds vodka. Get this down you, might even make you relax for once.'

'Oh just piss *off,* Ellie!'

The words exploded out of me before I thought them through. My hand flew to my mouth in momentary horror, but then a giggle worked its way through my fingers. Ellie's scandalised face as she regarded me was hilarious. Her expression suddenly changed to a snarl and she grabbed me by the arm.

'And to think I thought you were all right.' Ellie hissed, 'Should've known you were just like that slut, Olivia.'

I wrenched my arm out of her grasp. I staggered back a step, though I had not been drinking. I could still feel the press of her fingertips on my flesh. There would be bruises there tomorrow.

'You're a fake, Ellie.' I yanked her stupid tee shirt over my head and threw it at her feet. Ellie's eyes bulged. 'Olivia is worth ten of you.'

I turned on my bare feet, leaving her in my wake. I walked out on to the patio, my boots trailing from my hand. Niall stood near the sea wall, chatting with a friend. Knowing I had to act before I lost my nerve, I hopped up on the sea wall. Drawing level with them both, I tapped Niall on the shoulder. He turned, his gorgeous face close to mine.

His breath smelled of peppermint.

Before I could talk myself out of it, I pecked him on the lips like a knight would a princess in a fairy tale. 'Sorry.'

Niall grinned. 'For what?'

'For being so uptight all summer. For always rejecting you. For … well, everything. I cared what others thought of me so much, I never wondered what you thought of me.' I smiled, feeling free and hideously embarrassed, all at once.

'Well, that's my sister for you.' Niall shrugged. 'It's all about the image. But don't be too hard on her. She'll get it, eventually.'

Like I had to, I thought.

Then Niall grabbed me and pulled me close to him, landing his lips on mine. The music and rest of the party seemed to melt away, even the whoops and cheers of his friend nearby. I let myself lean against him, his warm body folded into mine. I could have stayed there all night, with him … But I needed to be someplace else.

I came up for air, opening my eyes. 'I have to go.'

'I'll come with you.' Niall said straight away.

'I've got to sort something out. I'll be back at the party later, okay?'

I took in Niall's uncertain face. I couldn't blame him thinking it might be an excuse.

'I promise, okay?'

Niall grinned and nodded. He helped me down as I hopped down from the sea wall. I had to untangle my hand from his as I walked away. Laughing, I turned to see Ellie and Vic watching me, their faces dark with fury. But for once, I didn't care. It all felt so toxic. Besides, when I came back to the party, I would be with Niall, not them and their fakery.

I gave them a little wave as I breezed past.

Six

As I wandered away from The Grange barely two hours after I'd arrived, I looked at my phone again. No messages. I had to pass the flat, so looked through the window: Mum was asleep on the sofa, the television still on. She hadn't even missed me. Parents!

Yawning, bone-weary, I walked the five minutes to Olivia's place. Jim's car was missing from the driveway. I went to the back first. Her curtains were drawn, the window shut. I went down the side and crept towards the planter where they kept the front door key: gone. I flashbacked to the week before: we'd used it then. Damn. I remembered Olivia putting it on her mess of a dressing table. I would bet money that it was still there, hidden amongst a tangle of jewellery, make-up and rubbish.

Hoping Jim's car wasn't in the garage and he was in after all, I rang the doorbell. A light came on in the porch. Olivia opened the door, a half-drunk bottle of whiskey in hand.

'Fuck off.' She said, slamming the door in my face.

I stood there, reeling. So, she definitely knew, then and had snubbed me at the party for sure. Thanks, Jenny! No, this was my fault. I had to take the consequences.

I tried ringing Olivia from the doorstep, but she hung up

on me. I rang the doorbell again. No answer.

'Olivia! Liv!' I pounded my fist on the door. 'I'm sorry!'

I leant on the doorbell, letting it ring and ring and ring.

Finally, Olivia's shadow appeared in the hallway. She wrenched the door open. She didn't take it off the security chain, so I couldn't get in.

'I told you … Don't you understand English?' She slurred.

I put my foot in the way and yelped with pain as she trapped it. 'Look, I get it. I'm an idiot. I should never have gone without you tonight … and I should have definitely told you!'

'Was it worth it?' Olivia spat. 'All summer you've been sucking up to Little Miss Popular. What about me? You've been putting me down, laughing at her jokes, excluding me …'

'… No. It wasn't like that. I swear down!'

But Olivia was on a roll. 'What is it like, then? Let me guess. Ellie says 'jump' and you ask, 'how high?' 'Cos that's what it's been all summer!'

'You're right. I've been a crap friend.'

Olivia was too drunk to process my admission. 'You're my best mate. You're supposed to stand up for me. We're a package deal, that's how it's meant to be!'

'It's true. Look, why don't you let me in?'

'Why should I?'

I couldn't answer that. I knew only too well that had I been the one without an invite, Olivia would have told Ellie where to go. She would have refused to go to the party on principle. I had made some of the right noises, but ultimately betrayed Olivia by going. Worst of all, I'd told myself it was no big deal, when I knew really it was.

'I'm sorry.' I said at last.

Olivia looked at me through the gap in the door, deflated. She slid down the hall wall, sitting on the floor. I sat down too, trying to get next to her, the stupid door still in the way. Olivia took another swig of whiskey. I recognised the label: it was her Dad's favourite, the one he'd been saving since his birthday. She'd be for it when he came home and found it gone. Drinking his stash was one of the only ways Olivia could get his attention.

'Go easy.' I noted how fast the whiskey was going down Olivia's throat.

'Oh, you care now?' Olivia was so drunk. I wondered how much more she'd had. She couldn't have got this pissed on the whiskey alone.

'Of course I care!' I retaliated. 'Look, I made the wrong choice. I know that now. Let me in, let's talk. Please?'

Olivia sighed. 'Whenever I've needed you lately, you've not been there.'

'… You mean this summer.'

'No … No, Jaz. Since we left school. It's not been the same.' Olivia took a juddering breath, tears tracking down her cheeks. 'We used to be so close. You were the only person who really understood. But lately … I've had no one.'

My mind swirled at my best friend's words. Could it be true? I felt sick, taking in the cool night air in big gulps. I thought of Niall, how much I'd liked him, yet how desperate I had been to try and impress Ellie. I'd kept him at arm's length, so why not Olivia too? I looked up at the dark sky. The stars seemed to spin around and around, coming on in at me.

'You're right. I'll change. I swear.'

Olivia knocked back yet more whiskey. In the time we'd

been talking, she must have drunk another third of the bottle. 'You know, she's been sending me messages.'

'Ellie has?'

'Yes, Ellie! Who else? I always get idiots trolling me online, but guess when it got even worse? When she got here.' Olivia laughed bitterly to herself. 'As if you didn't know. You probably wrote some of them, trying to get in with her.'

'No! No, of course not! I didn't. I give you my word, I didn't.'

Olivia regarded me through the gap in the door. 'Your word. Right. Not worth much.'

I couldn't argue with my best friend's logic on that one. I had let her down spectacularly. My eyelids grew heavy. I was so tired! Lack of food, training earlier and a long day had caught up with me. But I couldn't fall asleep sitting on my best friend's doorstep.

'Have I done something wrong? Have I done something to deserve this?'

I forced my eyelids open again. 'No … No.'

I tried to unclutter my thoughts. It was me who was weak. I was the one in the wrong. But words did not come to my lips. All I could see was Olivia's bottle, the stars, that darkness threatening to envelop me. I tried to keep my eyes open but then I blinked …

… And I was gone.

Seven

I came to with a jerk gasping, as if I'd surfaced from deep water.

I was still sitting on Olivia's doorstep, the dark night air above me. There was a sour taste in my mouth. My head throbbed dully, my joints stiff from sleeping sitting up. I was leaning against Olivia's front door. It was still ajar, the security chain on.

Instinctively, I looked first to my watch: one twenty in the morning. I was late for Mum's curfew, but hopefully she was still asleep. I pressed against the door to peer through, into Olivia's hallway. She was still there, passed out and slumped on the floor, the empty whiskey bottle discarded. The smell of vomit hung in the air. Even in the dim porch light I could see the ashen colour of Olivia's face.

Something was wrong.

I stretched out as far as I could and reached through the gap in the door. I managed to grab Olivia's prone leg. I took hold of her ankle and shook her as best I could.

'Olivia … Olivia! Wake up!'

No response. I had seen Olivia drunk and passed out many times, but I knew somehow this was different. Olivia was in serious trouble … And I couldn't get in. What now?

I found myself stumbling back down the high street, in the direction of The Grange. The music was turned down now, though it was still loud enough to be heard several doors down. I perceived, rather than saw, net curtains twitching as I made my way back, various locals' irritation at being kept up all night following me back.

I clambered up the steps onto The Grange's patio. Many of the teens had gone, drifting back to their homes. A handful of teens were scattered about the patio on large beanbags. Jake Harrington, asleep, his mouth opening and closing like a goldfish's. Andrew Franklin and Jenny Keller, curled up together on a sofa that had been dragged out from the living room. Ellie and Vic were on the swing seat next to the barbeque, heads together, murmuring to each other.

As I arrived on the patio, Niall appeared at the glass doors, hands on his hips, a look on his face that told me he thought I had blown him out earlier after all.

I didn't have time to explain. 'It's Olivia.'

~

'Have you rung for an ambulance?' Ste said, when I'd outlined what had happened. He'd been asleep in one of the upstairs bedrooms and been roused by Niall. Ste stood on the patio in pyjamas, his glasses on cock-eyed, looking more middle-aged than ever. Now we all looked to him, the only real adult there.

I shook my head dumbly. Ste raised his eyes skywards.

Ellie immediately grabbed for her mobile. 'I'll do it!'

Ste nodded at Niall, indicating his brother come with him. 'Come on,' He looked to me: 'Show us which house is hers.'

We hurried up the high street again, a strange sight: a young man in pyjamas followed by two teens holding hands. I felt like I was somehow out of my own body, looking down at us, the events unfurling.

We reached Olivia's house. Ste and Niall heaved the security chain out of the wood with co-ordinated shoulders against the door; the metal popped free with a clink, almost leaving them sprawling on the hall carpet. Barely noticing, Ste stumbled across the threshold into Jim's house and pressed an expert finger to Olivia's neck.

'She's got a pulse.' He confirmed.

'Ste's training to be a paramedic.' Niall said, by way of explanation.

I just shrugged, 'Oh'. What other response was there? There was so much I didn't know about the Macintoshes, I realised as I watched Ste check my best friend over. The brothers moved her from a pool of vomit, ensured her airways were clear, placed her in the recovery position. I fussed uselessly, fetching a blanket from the sofa in the living room, placing it over Olivia. Her lips and skin were tinged blue. I held her hand, noting how cold her flesh felt.

'Now what?' I said.

'We wait for the ambulance.' Ste was calm as ever.

'It's alcohol poisoning, isn't it.' I said, dread in my gut.

'Looks that way.' Niall eyed the empty whiskey bottle, which had now come to rest near the hall radiator.

'This is my fault.' I said.

'No one forced her to drink so much.' Ste countered.

I knew that was true, but Ste and Niall didn't know Olivia, or her life. I did. I was supposed to be the one person Olivia could lean on … But I'd decided to defect to the other side instead. I'd sucked up to Ellie like she was some kind of celebrity! I'd left Olivia out in the cold every time – or worse. No wonder the party had been the final straw.

The ambulance arrived with the shrill blare of sirens, drawing yet more Winby residents to their windows. Some even came out into the street in dressing gowns and onesies. Green jacketed paramedics with soothing voices told us they'd 'take it from here'.

My fault, my fault, my fault.

I watched, feeling hollow, hardly taking any of it in. Niall attempted to put an arm round my bare shoulders, but again I jerked away. Niall regarded me with that hurt look in his eye I had come to recognise so well. He thought I was rejecting him again, but it wasn't that. I didn't deserve his sympathy.

Jim's car pulled up at the house just as Olivia was being loaded on a gurney into the ambulance. Shocked, disbelieving, Jim left his car parked at an angle nearby and blundered towards the paramedics, asking the same question, over and over: *What's happened?* Ste tried to intervene and fill him in, but Jim merely made more demands: *Who the hell are you?* And then: *What have you done to my girl?*

A familiar face, I was pushed forward to reason with Jim. I persuaded him to let the paramedics do their jobs, to go with Olivia to the hospital in Exmorton. Jim seemed to shut down as I spoke to him, turning his back on me, clambering into the ambulance after Olivia. I tried to do the same, but the doors were slammed in my face as the sirens started up again and my best friend was transported out of Winby without me.

'I'll take you.' Niall said.

'You can't, you'll still be over the limit.' Ste replied in an exasperated tone, as if his brother was a child. 'I'll take her.'

'Then I'm coming too!' Niall said, eager as ever to compete with his brother.

I didn't say anything, not even 'thank you'. All I could think of was Olivia.

Ste grabbed his car keys. 'Let's go.'

Eight

It wasn't until we reached Exmorton hospital I even noticed it was three in the morning. Mum would surely have realised I was gone by now? She was a bad sleeper. She'd check on me randomly during the night, like I was still a baby. I had awoken many times to find her sitting on the end of my bed and staring ahead, into the shadows, a far-away look on her face.

I looked at my phone. I had turned it onto silent mode when I reached the party and not turned it back again. The voicemail and text message icons were blinking. Each text varied in anger and fear as the night wore on, the last one reading, *'OH JAZ PLEASE COME BACK DON'T STAY AWAY COZ U THINK U R IN TROUBLE I LOVE U JUST WANT TO KNOW WHERE U R XXX'.*

Mum must really be panicking if she wasn't using any punctuation. I had seen her on many occasions writing on blackboard menus and on shop signs. She would always remember to put apostrophes where they were needed, removing them when they were not. Conscious of the warnings in the hospital pointing out the dangers of mobile phones interfering with medical equipment, I dashed off a quick text to Mum, telling her something had happened to Olivia and

I would be back soon.

I walked into the accident and emergency department of the hospital, Niall and Ste flanking me like bodyguards. White tiles and plastic chairs, sick and injured people draped over them, looking bored and miserable. There was no receptionist at the counter, but a stern-looking male nurse took our enquiry and directed us to a relative's room when he heard who we were looking for.

'They're working on her now.' He said.

They're working on her now. It sounded so ominous and yet so humdrum, like they did this sort of thing every day. They probably did. To them, Olivia was just another daft kid who'd drunk too much. The doctors and nurses would do whatever they did to save her life, then go for drinks themselves after work, or home to their families. Wives and husbands would ask, 'Did you have a nice day?' and those doctors and nurses would smile and shrug and then ask what was for dinner.

But Olivia was a real person, not just a daft kid. She was the only one who knew me or my life, too. But so eager to impress Ellie, I'd let Olivia go with barely a second's thought. I had undervalued and let her down in equal measure.

I paced the waiting room. 'How long are they going to take!'

'It takes as long as it takes.' Ste said, with maddening simplicity.

I wanted to have a go at him; to say it must be nice to be him up on Mount Ste, looking down at the rest of us mere mortals.

'She'll be okay.' Niall said quietly.

How would you know, I wanted to demand. But didn't.

As usual.

At last a doctor appeared. She was young, she can't have been qualified long. Clipboard in hand, she wore a shiny stethoscope around her neck like it was expensive jewellery. Her white coat was pressed within an inch of its life.

'You can see her now.'

Oh, thank God.

I strode through to the curtained cubicles, grabbing good news and running with it, before bad news could follow me. Ste and Niall hung back. *Cubicle four,* the doctor said. *She had a close call, but she will be all right. Just make sure she never drinks as much again, okay?*

But the doctor – and all her colleagues who'd 'worked on' Olivia – had never met Olivia conscious. If she ever wanted to drink as much again, there would not be a thing I could do to stop her. Drawing back the curtain of cubicle four, I saw my best friend hooked up to a rehydration drip. Her skin was a terrible grey colour. Something told me she would not be repeating the episode.

'How are you?' I sat down next to her bedside on a hard, plastic chair. 'Where's your Dad?'

Olivia seemed confused. Her eyelids closed and opened again, as if she was working hard to stay awake. She looked to the other side of the bed.

'He … he was here a moment ago.' She took a deep breath. 'Coffee.' She said, like she was suddenly remembering something. 'Yeah. He went to get a coffee.'

I reached forward for her hand. She left it in mine for a few moments. Her skin was still deathly cold to touch. I remembered reading somewhere alcohol reduced a person's body temperature.

'I'm really sorry, Olivia.'

'What for?' Olivia seemed genuinely bewildered.

For a moment my heart lifted. Could we forget about it all, go back to normal, just like that? Had I learnt my lesson? But then I sighed. I couldn't just leave it. I owed it to Olivia, after everything I had (not) done, to fall on my sword.

'For everything.' I said.

Nine

Twenty minutes later and I emerged from the cubicle, choking back sobs, tears shining in my eyes.

It's too late, Olivia had said.

Our friendship was over.

Niall and Ste were out of the relatives' room now, sitting in those hard plastic chairs in front of the still empty reception. They were next to a cheerful man who held wadded bandages around his left hand, trying not to drip blood on the white floor. Ste and Niall were nodding as the man told them all about his accident.

'DIY.' The man said. 'I know what you're thinking … Why do DIY at night? Can't sleep, you see. Might as well use those hours constructively, right?'

'Right.' Ste echoed, actually looking as if he was paying attention.

Niall jumped to his feet as soon as he saw me however, betraying his own lack of interest. He clocked my upset immediately, but perhaps remembering how I'd lead him on then rejected him again the day before, he hung back.

'… Okay?' Niall enquired.

I nodded hastily, anxious not to look him in the eye. If I did, I was sure I'd start bawling. We walked out in silence to the car. Ste had got a parking ticket for not 'paying and displaying' properly. Ste let loose a few uncharacteristic profanities and ordered us both into the car. Even looking at Niall's smirk was not enough to raise a smile on my own face.

Ste dropped me outside the flat. I let myself in to discover Mum had spent most of the night pacing and calling everyone in Winby. She'd even called Kevin, wondering if I had gone in search of him. He had not been impressed. *You can't just call when you have a problem Linda*, he'd said. And he had a point: what was he to us, now?

'I don't understand.' Mum stared at me, still in my party clothes, though now they smelled of vomit. 'What have I done wrong? Why are you being like this?'

'It's not about you.' I said, surprising myself. Normally I just kept quiet and let Mum rant at me: *it's about respect. You earn your privileges. I ask so little of you.* Blah, blah blah. Hands off parenting … Yeah, that worked out so well.

'Then what is it about!' Mum shrieked.

'You wouldn't understand.'

'Try me.'

But I just stood there, silent, meeting Mum's gaze. She soon tired of me.

'Oh … Get out of my sight, Jasmine.'

I was grounded. Knowing nothing about what happened to Olivia, Mum threw extra chores at me. I had to cook dinner every night and she even told me I couldn't meet friends for the remaining two weeks of the holiday. This meant I didn't see Ellie or her family again, only receiving a 'Bye xx' text message from Niall. The Mackintoshes packed up The Grange, which I heard from Jenny Keller. I did what I was supposed to, serving my grounding with good grace. It was the only way to regain Mum's trust.

Olivia and I had fallen out before, but only for a few days here and there. Now it had been weeks since I last heard from my best friend. I sent text after text, but received no reply. I tried ringing; emailing; sending private messages on Instagram. She didn't reply to any of them.

There was one place Olivia couldn't avoid me: the college bus. I knew pinning all my hopes on that was not a great idea, but I hoped that by taking my usual seat on the bus in the morning for college, Olivia would come and sit next to me, just like old times. Surely Olivia had made me pay enough? She *had* to forgive me.

I awoke with butterflies in my stomach. I ate a quick breakfast, grabbing my books and bag. I ran down to the seafront for the bus, certain I would see Olivia puffing after me. Yet my road was silent. A group of teens were gathered at the clock tower as usual, grumbling, as if the summer hadn't even happened.

Olivia wasn't amongst them. Was she late, even on the very first day? Typical. The bus arrived and we all clambered on board, paying the driver as we did so. I took up my usual space, two rows from the back, by the window. Olivia would arrive …

… Any. Minute. Now.

The Driver stuck the bus in gear and the engine revved, so he might turn the vehicle around the clock tower and go back up the long high street and out towards Exmorton. But he was leaving without Olivia!

'Wait … Wait!'

The Driver's eyes looked back at me, bored, from the rear view mirror. The previous term we'd had a woman driver who'd listened to Metallica and Guns N' Roses on the bus' ancient cassette player, probably the only means of transport left in the universe with one. She'd had blood-red fingernails and dyed black hair. This new guy was much younger, but was somehow more middle-aged, his hair already thinning on top. He looked like Ste would in fifteen years.

'There's still one more?' I called.

'Who?' A head bobbed up from the back row, next to Jake Harrington and Andrew Franklin. It was Jenny Keller. Who else?

'Olivia.'

'She's left college.' Jenny delivered this devastating news coolly, messing with her phone as she did so.

I couldn't believe it. 'Wh-why? When did this happen?'

'She got a job or something.' Jake offered, shrugging. How could he know this and I didn't!

'What? Where?' I demanded.

'London. I think. Her Mum got it for her.' Jenny smiled at me. 'Want to sit with us?'

I declined, trying to process this information as the bus sped out of Winby and towards Exmorton. Olivia had meant it. Our friendship *was* over. In trying to be cool and popular like Ellie, now I was alone.

With not much else to do, I knuckled down to my studies and running. I missed out on county level again, but I saw Olivia's life grow on Instagram as mine became smaller. Her profile revealed she was living with a family in London as a nanny, looking after two small boys for a family who seemed to travel all over the world. Olivia's photographs showed her in ever more exotic places. Her affection for the children was obvious. She was doing well. She was out in the world and discovering it. She'd realised she was important. Finally.

In contrast, I came home from college and did my home-work every night in Teddy's, waiting for Mum to finish over the road at Flossie's. I watched Jenny Keller, Jake Harrington and Andrew Franklin together. I'd only ever wanted to be popular. Instead I remained the outsider, on the edge of things, left behind.

Then one night, I opened my books and closed them again. I had been punished enough for letting Olivia down. She had moved on, so would I.

Feeling the weight of the boys' stares as I approached the table, I greeted Jenny with a large smile. She matched it with one of her own. Then I took a deep breath and said a phrase I'd been practicing, over and over, in my head for weeks, yet had not had the nerve to try. Until now.

'Mind if I join you?' …

Stalk

'You don't lose when you lose fake friends.'
Joan Jett

Ten

Saturday, August 25th

… Something changed. I perceived, rather than heard, the door to the café open. The bell above tinkled as a breeze swept in with whoever it was. A shiver went down my spine and I blinked, looking around me in confusion.

'Jasmine, you okay?'

Jenny Keller looked up at me from her table, head tilted. Andrew Franklin and Jake Harrington sat with her, though they were ignoring me. For a moment, I felt certain I was about to sit down with them. But that made no sense. We weren't friends, never had been. Embarrassment seized me.

'Yes, 'course.' I muttered, moving away before Jenny could say anything else. I could see her shrug in my peripheral vision. I turned back towards the counter.

Mum was standing too close, behind me. I jumped, then sighed. So, it had been her coming into Teddy's.

'Hello my favourite child.' Mum grinned at me. There was red lipstick on one of her teeth. God, she was so embarrassing.

I rolled my eyes. 'I'm your only child. What are you

doing here, stalking me?'

'Can't a woman get a coffee?' Mum's tone was jokey. This was going to be even worse than I thought.

I folded my arms. 'You always say buying coffees is a waste of money when you can get a whole jar of instant for the same price.'

Mum nodded. 'Okay, you got me. I came in to check you were still okay to make dinner tonight? Otherwise I won't have time to eat between finishing at Flossie's and going up to clean at the caravan park.'

My heart sank. I'd forgotten all about it. 'I'm going out …'

Mum's demeanour changed in an instant. She seemed to sag, like I'd let all the air out of her. 'Jaz, I ask so little of you …'

'I know, I know.' I was anxious to stop the fight in its tracks, especially considering we were in public. 'I'll do it. I promise.'

It was not like me to roll over so quickly. Mum's eyes narrowed as she regarded me. 'You didn't mention anything about going out before? I thought you had training with the harriers tomorrow.'

'It's last minute,' I said, truthfully. Then lying through my teeth: 'It's just a small thing.'

'My 'Mum Sense' is tingling.' Mum declared.

'Mum! For God's sake.' I glanced around just in case anyone heard her. Mum was always saying daft things like that. 'Why do you always think there has to be something going on?'

'Because usually there is.'

'There isn't.' I insisted.

Mum looked me up and down, clearly not believing me.

And wasn't she right?

'Okay,' she said at last. 'Olivia's going too?'

I nodded, too fast. Mum's lips pursed in disapproval.

'I knew it.' Mum sighed. 'You've been acting furtive for weeks. This is about that grockle girl on the seafront, isn't it?'

'She's called Ellie,' I hissed, guiding Mum towards an empty chair. I didn't want Jenny Keller eavesdropping any more than she had already. 'She hasn't invited Olivia to the party, that's all. No biggie.'

'So why don't you or Olivia ask if it's okay she goes?' Mum plopped down in the chair with a sigh, like all adults do. My glum face gave her the confirmation she needed. ' … Ah. I get it. This girl doesn't like Olivia and doesn't want her to come … And now you feel awkward, so you have been avoiding Olivia all day.'

I shrugged. 'What else am I supposed to do?'

'How about stand up to this girl?'

'I can't.'

'Can't or won't?' Mum raised her eyebrows at me.

I grabbed the menu, averting my eyes from hers. 'It's not as simple as that.'

'Isn't it?' Mum said, as infuriating as ever.

'It's the biggest party of the year!' I said, 'Why should I miss out?'

Mum grinned, delighted to catch me out. 'I thought it was just a small thing? Besides, isn't Olivia your best friend?'

Argh! Didn't Mum know answering questions with questions was rude? In fact, she had taught me that! Mum never played by the rules.

'Olivia's hardly gone out of her way to make this girl

welcome, you know.' I mumbled, 'It's her fault she's being left out.'

'If you say so, hun.' Mum sighed.

I waited, sure there was more coming. *Yup …*

'… You know, there once was a time the Jasmine I know wouldn't have even had to make a choice. It would have been automatic she chose her best friend.'

I hated it when Mum referred to me in the third person, usually because it meant she was right. But I wasn't going to admit that.

'So, do you want a drink or not?' Mum said, after thirty seconds of me eyeballing her in silence.

'Not.' I rose from my seat.

Mum was smirking, like I amused her. 'Bye then!'

I hesitated a second, sure Mum would tell me to sit back down. But she didn't. Mum called after me as I trudged outside:

'And don't forget dinner!'

I stood at the seafront, looking down on to the beach. It was a grey August day, more like October. I shivered again, remembering the weird sensation in Teddy's when the door opened and the bell rang. Like *deja vu*. But what had I been expecting? I wouldn't have joined Jenny at the table with the boys, why would I? It was odd to see Mum in the café, but not exactly unheard of; she only worked over the road. I sighed and watched the tide going out, each time retreating further and further out into the cove.

'Oi, oi.' Olivia's voice sounded behind me. I turned to see my best friend, a tray of chips in hand. She speared one with a wooden fork and held it out to me: 'Chip?'

'Thanks.' I took one and blew on it. 'What you doing here?'

Olivia shoved another chip in her mouth. 'Where else would I be, but this dump?'

Truth. Winby was beautiful, but boring. Nothing ever happened here. The most exciting thing that had happened all summer was Ellie and her family moving into The Grange. Olivia and I had made plans all year to have a real blow out, a summer of fun. Instead we'd been bored out of our brains, bingeing boxsets on Netflix and scrolling through our phones. The usual. We never had the money to do anything else.

'So, there's a party tonight at Ellie's, apparently.'

Olivia's words brought my attention back with a jolt. Ellie in her pyjamas speared through my brain; what she'd told me this morning when I'd gone for a run. The Snapchat message. *You tell her or I will.* It had seemed so simple this morning: I would tell Olivia about the party and how she wasn't invited, because it would be so much worse coming from the new girl. I took a deep breath.

'Oh, that. I thought I'd have an early night?'

Lies. Why was I lying!

'But it's Saturday?' Olivia said, as if I was an idiot.

'I've got training in the morning.'

That much at least was true. I was keen to improve on my time and get into the county squad. I'd missed out by seconds the year before.

'Okay, well if you're not going, I won't bother.'

I breathed a sigh of relief. 'It's the holidays, every night's like Saturday night, we could do something tomorrow night instead.'

I could feel a strange hot sensation creeping up my neck. I hated lying to Olivia. I prayed I wasn't going red. She'd bust me then for sure.

Yet Olivia seemed oblivious. 'Sure, tomorrow then?'

'Fine.' I breathed a sigh of relief as I watched her throw her chip paper in the overflowing bin by the seafront. She gave me a quick hug and was on her way again.

I'd got away with it.

Eleven

I traipsed back to the flat and went straight to my room. I grabbed my phone from my pocket as I flung myself down on my bed. I typed out a text to Niall, *Looking forward to the party tonight? xx* and sent it.

Almost immediately, a reply came: *SURE*.

Niall always wrote texts in capitals. No kisses. That didn't mean he was going off me … Did it? Suddenly I felt even more dejected.

I wavered, thinking about calling up Olivia's profile and telling her I was going to the party after all. What was the worst Ellie could do, if I turned up with Olivia that night? She might tell us both to leave, but surely Niall would tell us to stay … He was my boyfriend. Except, was he? I wasn't sure what that meant. Maybe he was just tolerating me because I was hanging out with his sister.

I typed out another text to Niall, *See you there xxx*

I waited for the reply. None came. Well, it didn't really need a reply, did it? He didn't mean anything by it. Did he? I hated being so uncertain of everything.

Maybe all I needed to do was grab Niall's attention. '*Dress code: Fabulous*' Ellie had instructed. I hadn't a clue what she meant by this. Shifting through my wardrobe and drawers it was soon apparent I hadn't got anything even remotely 'fabulous' enough for a party. I thought back to Ellie's stupid teenage magazines, all the advice they gave out on being a fashion icon. When all else fails, wear black, is what they said (whoever 'they' actually were).

Rifling through my clothes I found a pair of black jeans in the bottom of my chest of drawers. I hadn't worn them in ages. They'd been too tight at the waist after I had scoffed my face at Christmas. But I'd done lots of training since then, I must be slimmer now. I shimmied them on. My hunch was right, I could now fasten the zip. But I'd also grown in the last eight months: they now flapped around the ankle. *Typical.*

Single-minded, I strode back into the kitchen, grabbing a pair of scissors. I cut the denim, then ripped each leg off. I pulled them back on. Black hot pants. *Perfect.*

I turned my chest of drawers out, looking for my black vest top. Mum can't have put a wash on since last weekend. Sigh. I pulled the lid off my bulging washing basket. Sure enough, there it was at the top. I picked it up and sniffed it. Seemed OK, but there were deodorant white marks on the underarms.

In just my bra and the hot pants, I went back out into the kitchen and sponged at the marks, getting the worst off. I pulled the vest top over my head, trying to ignore the dampness on my underarms. I couldn't. I raced into Mum's room and grabbed her hairdryer, plugging it in and focusing it on the damp patches, burning my skin and swearing in the process.

Finally, the top was dry. I regarded myself in my Mum's full-length mirror. I saw for the first time how thin I was, how angular my elbows and knees looked. Being thin was all teen mags and sites ever seemed promote, but all I could see was the body of a child. Where were my boobs, my bum? An ugly rash of freckles were scattered over the bones of my sternum, there was a large bruise from training on the back of my left calf. I looked at my hands and feet; my bitten nails and cracked toenails. *Ugh.*

I opened my mother's dressing table drawers, pulled out some make-up, lipstick, nail polish. I could reinvent myself. Niall would not be able to believe it!

Twenty-five minutes later, I stood in front of the mirror again. There was a vague improvement. My freckly face was now smooth and porcelain-like. I'd ever put foundation and powder on my chest. I borrowed a chunky red shell necklace of my Mum's and pulled on my red boots. A touch of red lipstick and matching red nails finished off the look. Was I 'fabulous', like Ellie had commanded?

Near enough, I decided.

' ... Jaz?'

I heard Mum before I saw her. Something nagged at the back of my mind. Wasn't I meant to have done something by the time she got back?

'Why isn't the dinner on!' Mum shouted through.

Oh. That.

I moved out of Mum's room, steeling myself for the inevitable onslaught. 'Sorry ...!'

Mum didn't look at me, she was too busy talking to herself. '... Don't know why I bother!' She made a point of opening and slamming cupboard doors, looking for something for us to eat. 'It's not like I didn't remind you ... '

Her words trailed off. Finally, she looked at me. And stopped dead.

Mum's mouth opened and shut. For once, she was actually lost for words. I fought down a triumphant smile. I'd never seen her like that before.

Her surprise turned to dark fury. 'What the hell are you wearing?'

'It's on trend.' I declared, as if that was an explanation.

'I don't care if it's 'on trend'! For God's sake Jaz, I ask so little of you … And you want to go out dressed like a slut?'

'I think I look nice.' I said quietly.

Mum sat down at the table. Her head was in her hands as if she couldn't support the weight of it. 'I've been at work all day, I have to go out to my second job any minute now, I have a terrible headache … I don't need this, Jaz.'

'You never do!'

Time froze the moment I said those words. Our eyes locked in that second: her betrayal, my anger, all mixed up together, ready to explode. Of course she didn't need a teenage daughter starting on her the moment she got back after an eight hour day! But then, I didn't need a mother who was always working, chasing after every last penny, either. I wanted a mother who was free to involve herself in my life, *properly*. To hell with money! I wanted it to be like when I was small, when everything was so much simpler, when she could fix everything. I just wanted my Mum.

'You're grounded. Go and get changed.'

'Mum …' I started, an apology ready.

'… Now!'

I stomped off to my room, slamming the door, daring her to come after me. I waited a few seconds before I realised she wasn't going to. I stood in the middle of my bedroom, undecided.

I could do what Mum wanted: take off my party gear, get into my pyjamas, then go back out into the kitchen and cook dinner. Or I could stay and sulk in my room. I knew that if I did either, Mum would hold no grudge: we could go back to normal the next day, just like that. But maybe that concept of 'normal' was no longer enough?

I was sick of doing what I was told.

Twelve

First, preparation. Mum would be going to work in the next half an hour, but I needed to get going. I was already late. She probably wouldn't even look in to my room before she went, but just in case I had to make sure I didn't get busted.

I reached forward to my tablet and turned YouTube on low. I'd seen an old movie once where the protagonist had set up an elaborate system of pulleys. This meant when people opened his bedroom door, it looked as if he was in bed, breathing. I didn't have a clue how to do this though, so I grabbed some dirty clothes and stuffed my bed up with them, as if I was in it. That would have to do.

I looked around my room one last time. Then to the window, my means of escape: *was I really going to do this?*

I couldn't breathe. The air felt like it was splitting apart. I felt hot and tingly. I took a deep breath, but it failed to reach my lungs. Gulping another in, I sat back down on my bed. Who was I kidding? I was no rebel. The most daring thing I'd ever done on purpose was walk across the pedestrian crossing at Union Street when it was still amber!

As if in answer, my phone rang. I grabbed it and looked at the screen. On it, Olivia's name and picture flashed.

'Hello?'

'Jaz.' Olivia's voice seemed strange, far away. 'I've been thinking ... Why don't you come over tonight, after all?'

Irritation coursed through me. I was trying to work up the courage to disobey my mother for the first time in my life! *Well, it wasn't always about Olivia.*

'I told you I can't.'

There was a pause as Olivia digested my curt reply. 'Please Jaz.'

Something definitely sounded different about her, but I was too bothered by my argument with Mum to decode what.

'I'm grounded.' That much was the truth.

'Grounded! But you're such a square! What for?' Olivia sounded both relieved and incredulous, if that was even possible.

'Oh, long story.' I said. 'Tell you tomorrow.'

'Okay.' Olivia said, sounding unsure again. 'See you then.'

''Bye.' I rang off.

I looked at the window. Our flat was on the ground floor of the converted house we lived in. All I had to do was open it and slip out into the summer night air, leaving it on the latch. Yet somehow it felt like a huge undertaking.

'I ask so little of you ...' Mum always said.

Guilt stabbed at me. It was true. She worked all the hours and still did everything around the house, asking me only to make the odd dinner when she was out past six. Was it really so much to ask?

But let's turn it around, my inner child said, shouting over my more reasonable side. Had I really ever done anything that bad? Bar the occasional (accidental) incident of drunkenness, Mum had the model teenage daughter.

When most teens were partying or behaving badly, I could be found studying for college or training for county level. What was one party? Even if she busted me, it would be just one incident. Other parents had a multitude of troubles thrown at them by their teens. I was not a problem child! I deserved to have some fun. Besides, I needed to see Niall and keep Becky Jarvis away from him.

I *was* going to the party.

I opened the window. I climbed up on the sill and looked back at my bedroom door, daring it to open. It didn't. So Mum wasn't superhuman, for all the times she'd declared her 'Mum sense was tingling' in that uber-embarrassing way of hers!

I hesitated before I jumped, cautious as ever. But it was only a two-foot drop, if that. Below my window, the street. Bins and recycling boxes lay discarded, leaflets for various takeaways and cans, glass bottles and plastics spilling onto the concrete. I jumped down, avoiding the detritus below and reaching up, closing the window without re-catching the latch, so I might sneak in later.

Sneak in later, I marvelled, barely recognising myself.

Looking back over my shoulder all the way down the road, I took the long way around. I practically ran all the way to the high street, only slowing down to bob down a side alley to avoid going past Olivia's. I checked my phone intermittently as I went: no texts from Mum, demanding I came back that instant. I was almost disappointed, though I wasn't sure why.

Music was pounding from The Grange and up the high street. Partygoers meandered down past Flossie's and The Penguin Fish Bar. I slowed down, feigning nonchalance as Jake Harrington nodded 'hello' on his way past. He was wearing black trousers and a tie, carrying a twelve pack of beer. Perhaps he had come straight from work? I realised with a jolt I didn't have a bottle with me. Ellie would think that a huge faux pas!

I rifled through my pockets and found some coins, ducking into the mini market on Fore Street. I walked past the over-priced fresh produce and the overflowing baskets of sweets and chocolate, straight to the off-licence section at the back. I grabbed a plastic litre bottle of white cider. It would have to do; it was all I could afford.

I took it to the bored assistant at the counter, a young woman with a nose ring. She looked me up and down, then at the 'Think 21' sticker on the till but didn't say anything. She placed the bottle in a thin carrier bag, holding out a hand for my money. Silently, I handed it over and grabbed the bag, scuttling out before she could give me my penny change or change her mind.

More partygoers were wandering past the mini market, so I fell into step with them. I didn't recognise most of them and none of them were dressed like me. They all looked like they were going to a wedding. What the hell?

I looked for someone, anyone I knew, the plastic bag with the cider banging against my bare legs. Though a couple of teens nodded at me, recognising me from college, there was no one I could call a friend. For a moment, I thought about calling Olivia, but what if that meant Ellie wouldn't let us in? That would be super embarrassing. I was only thinking of Olivia. Besides, Niall would be at the party. I could talk to him when I got there.

I kept walking.

Thirteen

The doors to The Grange were open. Teens clambered up on to the patio rather than walk round to the front door. On it, underneath the balcony, was Ellie. She wore her hair up, fixed tight with a thousand grips and probably five hundred millilitres of hairspray. But it was her dress I was transfixed by: a ballgown.

Ellie was wearing a ballgown.

It was beautiful: blue with a sparkling bustier, there was layer after layer of crinkly material underneath, making her look like one of Disney's Princesses … Or one of those dolls that go on the top of the loo roll in the bathroom. I stared down at my own outfit, non-plussed.

'Jasmine!' Ellie swooped on me, doing air kisses next to each of my cheeks. 'What happened to your trouser legs! Lose them on the way here?'

'They're hot pants.' I muttered, humiliation pricking at me. I had felt sure my outfit would get Ellie's approval. But I could never get it right, could I?

But Ellie wasn't listening. A super-thin girl I hadn't noticed was standing nearby, smoking a green cocktail cigarette in a holder. An actual holder. I noticed the colour of both matched her dress: a kind of sludgy dark green power suit that made her bony shoulders look like a coat-hanger.

'Jaz, this is my friend Victoria. Victoria's from London, too.'

'Hi.' I said, shyly.

Victoria barely looked at me, extending a hand with cool indifference. For a moment I wondered if I was supposed to kiss it. We shook hands instead, her skin felt cold. I looked behind me, sure Victoria must be looking at someone else on the patio. Instead, she was looking out to sea, as if everyone and everything surrounding her, including Ellie, bored her.

'Jaz is the one I was telling you about, Vic?'

Despite the ballgown, Ellie looked different somehow. Earnest. Smaller. I was confused. Was this what I looked like, when talking to Ellie?

'The runner. Right.' Victoria plucked the cigarette stub from the end of the holder and ground it beneath one killer heel on the patio. 'I'd run too, if I lived here. Away.' She cracked a smile at last, believing herself to be terribly droll.

Ellie tittered. 'Good one.'

'Is Niall around?' I was desperate to get away from them both.

Deep in conversation, neither Ellie or Victoria replied. I hovered, unsure if I was supposed to leave, or wait for them to answer. After forty or fifty uncomfortable seconds, irritation got the better of my desire to be courteous.

'Bye then!'

Neither of them noticed I was gone.

I wandered across the patio. Teens were draped everywhere: on the sea wall, the prized deck chairs (grabbed the moment they were vacated) and even on the unlit barbeque block. I saw faint recognition in various people's eyes, but it was obvious no one really knew who I was. *Great.*

I grabbed a drink and floated about, in the hope I might find Niall. But The Grange was so large, it soon became apparent I might be walking around in circles all night. Twenty minutes later and no closer to finding him, I decided to go back outside and wait on the patio. He had to turn up there sometime … Right?

Dusk was arriving as I arrived back outside. It was that pale grey light that makes everyone squint, in-between day and night. Everyone's faces were shadowy, making it difficult to know who you were talking to until you went right up next to them. Bored, I unscrewed the plastic bottle top off the cider and took a long swig. I hadn't eaten dinner – I'd forgotten to cook it, after all –so the alcohol went straight to my head as it worked its way down into my stomach. I felt instantly drunk … and a little bit sick. I hated cider. But it was better than just standing there like an idiot as the party went on around me.

In a world of my own, I exactly wasn't sure when Nat Williams appeared out of the darkness next to me, smoking a cigarette. He was just suddenly there, chatting and puffing.

'Are you talking to me?' I slurred.

'You'll do.' Nat winked. 'Great party, yeah?'

No it's not, I thought.

But then Nat was the stereotypical life and soul of the party. People were literally attracted to him like he was some kind of magnet, boys and girls alike. I had never really spoken to him before; all I'd known about him was he'd once gone out with Jenny Keller but cheated on her with Olivia. Olivia had not said much about him (or his performance), but Nat's reputation preceded him. Everyone always had something good to say about him: *Nat's a laugh.*

Nat's a good bloke. I wondered how I could be thought of like that. I'd probably need a whole personality transplant.

Nat chatted away at me. I watched his lips moving. Drunk and slow, I could barely hear what he was saying above the music. After asking him to repeat himself a few times, I was too embarrassed to ask anymore. I just interjected with various 'yeahs' and 'sures' wherever I thought I should. It seemed to be working. Then he stopped and grinned at me, stroking my arm.

'You're really pretty.'

Nat was a huge guy, easily six four. A rugby player. He was seen as one of the most eligible guys at college. For a microsecond, I forgot all about Niall. I couldn't quite believe Nat Williams was talking to me. Before I could answer, someone else appeared on the other side of me.

Jenny Keller. *Of course.* What the hell was she doing … Maybe she was the one stalking me this summer?

'She's fine, thanks!'

Jenny grabbed my elbow, attempting to steer me away from Nat. Absurdly, he grabbed my other arm, as if I were a ragdoll they were fighting over. Stronger than us both, I could feel his rough palms on my upper arm.

'I think she can answer for herself.' Nat's face was deadpan. All of a sudden, I felt intimidated by him. But Nat was a good bloke. Everyone said so.

Jenny did not let her gaze waver from his, nor did she let me go.

'We've got things to talk about, haven't we Jaz?' She said through gritted teeth. For reasons I did not understand, I somehow knew she wanted me to agree with her. 'She'll come find you later Nat, okay?'

Nat's cold eyes fixed on me. I smiled hesitantly, not sure

what I had caught myself in the middle of, yet desperate to extract myself.

'Right.' I said.

Nat cracked a grin at this, finally letting his grip on my arm drop. His smile, complete with perfect teeth, lit up his face. It was not difficult to see why he was so popular with all the girls. Yet in that microsecond with Jenny, I had glimpsed something else in him too: something disconcertingly steely. As if he was used to getting what he wanted and to hell with anyone who got in his way.

But then the moment seemed to pop, like a soap bubble. Any pressure I'd felt vanished as he melted back into the crowd, leaving me sure I had imagined it all.

I rounded on Jenny. 'What the hell was that?'

'Don't be alone with him.' Jenny declared. 'I mean it, Jaz!'

Even though I had no interest in Nat, I felt myself bristle. Jenny was swaying visibly. She was drunk. And jealous! For God's sake. All of this was so pointless. As I looked around the patio, faces seemed to leer in at me in my own drunken state.

I had to get out of there.

Giving up finding Niall, I turned away from Jenny for the second time that day, forcing my way across the patio and back into the house. Suddenly the lights on in the living room flickered and the music turned off. Indignant teen voices echoed through the air.

Before I even made it into the kitchen and heard her voice, I knew who was responsible. It was all so inevitable.

I braced myself and opened the kitchen door.

Fourteen

' … For God's sake, don't make a scene, Livvy!' Ellie was advancing on Olivia in the kitchen as I made it through the door.

'That's. Not. My. Name!' Olivia was wild-eyed, two wires in hand. She'd unplugged the extension lead that lead from the speakers in the kitchen to the massive stereo in the living room.

My best friend hadn't seen me yet. Curious teens gathered behind me. Some were muttering, others watching with baited breath as the events unfurled around us.

Ellie folded her arms. 'I didn't think you would want to come.'

'I didn't!'

'Then what's the problem!'

' … Oh, there she is!' Olivia turned away from Ellie, who was not used to such treatment. The new girl's eyes bulged at the dismissal.

'Let's go home and talk about this.' In Olivia's sights at last, I took in my best friend. She was swaying, drunk. And very, very angry. A dangerous combination.

'Talk about what?' Olivia demanded. 'That you're supposed to be my friend, but you're here, stabbing me in the back?'

A nervous titter made its way through the small crowd on the balcony above us. A tall lad, Jay Something - he was in my Science class - attempted to grab the cord off Olivia. But she laughed and danced out of his reach.

Olivia curled her lip at me. 'Look at you. Bet it's nice being one of the cool kids, eh?'

I couldn't argue with that. It had been exactly what I wanted. Only now, I could see it wasn't worth it. I'd wanted to be cool, popular like Ellie. Accepted. But Olivia had always made me feel that.

'I didn't mean anything by it.' I winced as these words came out. So, what had I meant?

Olivia let Jay have the cord at last. 'So you just sold me out all summer for no reason?'

He grabbed it and plugged it back in. The others drifted away as the music started blaring again. It was ridiculously cheerful against the face/off of me and Olivia, with Ellie and Vic on the sidelines, arms folded and indignant.

'Just … go, will you? Nobody wants you here!' Ellie exclaimed.

But Olivia didn't care what Vic or Ellie thought. 'You were supposed to be different, Jaz. Guess that's all done with, now.'

Panic flooded my chest. Surely Olivia couldn't be serious? Our friendship could not be over just because I'd chosen to go to the party! Then I remembered Mum's words: *There once was a time the Jasmine I knew wouldn't have to make a choice.* I was not worthy. I was a truly crap friend.

'Oh for … What is it with this melodrama!' Ellie declared, eyes rolling. 'She came to the party, you weren't invited. Get over it.'

'Is that what it was?' Olivia challenged me. 'Did you think of me at all?'

I stared back at my best friend, still caught between her and Ellie. I didn't know what to say. I felt embarrassment prickle through me, a red flush crept across my pale skin. Resentment flowered with it. Why did Olivia have to make things so difficult? Why did she always have to make a scene! Had I thought of her? Of course, but I had gone anyway. Surely it was worse to admit that. Better I lie?

'No.' I was anxious for this to all be over.

My best friend's tense posture seemed to slacken. All light and fire in Olivia's eyes appeared to go out and I knew instantly I had made the wrong choice.

'I'm sorry...' I began.

'Whatever.' Olivia cut me dead. She shook her head, let out a little half-laugh. 'I should've known.'

'Sayonara, slapper!' Vic called as Olivia gave her the finger. I watched as my best friend wrenched open the back door and disappear outside. 'God. What is she like?'

'Oh, that's not even the half of it.' Ellie forced a chuckle out of her mouth. 'Jaz can tell you … Jaz? Jaz!'

But I wasn't listening anymore. I turned my back on Ellie and Vic. Pulling on my red boots as I went, I made my way across the kitchen, directly through a throng of teen boys sharing a joint by the pantry. I ignored one who grabbed at my bare leg, not even caring as they hooted at me. I knew Ellie was yelling after me, but I didn't look round. I just didn't care anymore what she thought.

I had to make it right with Olivia.

~

I strode up the high street to Olivia's. *I should have known*, Olivia said. Had she been waiting for this day? The time she would look to me for back up and I wouldn't be there? Well, if she had, she was right to be cautious. I had let her down, but not just tonight. For the whole summer. Probably before that.

I knocked once, but before I could retrieve the key from its hiding place, Jim opened the door, his face reddened by whiskey and his expression twice as sour.

'Whaddya want.' His voice was gruff. He'd been a good-looking man once, but now drink and life had ravaged him. Off-duty, he'd not shaved in days, or changed. Stains and crumbs littered his once white tee shirt.

'Olivia in?' I tried to speak and hold my breath at the same time; I didn't want to breathe his malodorous self in.

'Out.' He made to close the door again.

Before he could, I squeezed through the gap. 'I'll wait then.'

I was too close to him for my liking in the narrow hall. Olivia's bedroom was on the ground floor. There was a chance she'd clambered in through her window, rather than see Jim in this state.

'Suit yourself.' Jim shuffled back towards the sitting room. Seconds later, a clink of glass and the remote fired an action movie into life: he'd already forgotten I was in the house.

I padded through to Olivia's room, knocking softly. Even though there was no answer, I still expected to find her on the unmade bed, staring up at her posters. But she wasn't there. Her room seemed curiously quiet without her. I wasn't sure if I had been there alone before. Always her bedroom was full of music from her laptop, or noise from the television; often both. Cigarette stubs filled an ashtray and floated in half-full mugs. The acrid smell of smoke hung heavy in the air. Dirty washing, plates, pencils, magazines and books littered every surface and the floor. Her bed was a tangled mass of duvet and sheets. Her dressing table was almost undistinguishable beneath a mass of make-up: lipsticks, eyeliners and pots of foundation. Broken bronzer and blush palettes had spilt, sending sparkling dust over the mirror, an old landline phone and a jewellery box.

I sat there for about twenty minutes, sure she would show. When she didn't, I started phoning her. After the fifth time of leaving a message, I rang off and looked around the bedroom for inspiration. I strained to remember: had Olivia had a bag with her at Ellie's? I was pretty sure she hadn't: no bag meant no purse. She was barred from The Moon again, plus even if she'd some money in her pocket, it wouldn't have been enough to get a taxi into Exmorton and back. Olivia had been complaining she had no money to me the day before.

So where could she be?

I opened the jewellery box: bronzer smeared on my fingertips. Inside, a junk of broken chains and tarnished rings. But in one of the compartments: a cylindrical cat's eye. Olivia had kept it. I remembered that night. We had been about twelve and it had been a washout of a summer like this one. With no money and nowhere to go, we'd gone up to the old road. No cars went there now; the new road into Winby took all the traffic away. We'd wandered up there, in the middle of the tarmac, pretending we were in one of the post-apocalyptic films, the last humans in existence. When we'd become bored, we'd dug the old cats eyes out of their rubber sockets. It turned out they were cylindrical chunks of glass. I don't know what we were expecting.

There was an unbroken view across the bay from that height: the balustrade was crumbling away. There, against the backdrop of the headland, we'd suddenly realised how small we really were against the hugeness of nature, yet neither of us had been able to put it into words.

Olivia was on the old road.

I wasn't sure how I knew this, I just did. Perhaps it was the last remnants of our friendship bonding us.

I had to go to her now.

Fifteen

Rather than face Jim again, I pushed Olivia's window open and let myself out onto the street. I made my way back down the high street, cutting through that side alley past Teddy's. I made my way up to The Mount, the name for the headland that overlooked Winby. I dug my red boots into the cliff pathway, which was soft with rain. I made my way through the locals' short cut through the ridiculous flower arrangements, to the pathway up the headland.

There was a cliff railway on the other side, which only tourists used to go from the bottom of the cove to the top. It had barely run this summer: the weather was so bad, the tourists had stayed away. Installed by the Victorians an age ago, the cliff railway stood idle, its massive levers locked and padlocked. Next to it the coastguard phone, the cable hung uselessly, its receiver missing. Twilight gave everything a greyish glow, the light of the moon sinking behind yet more dark cloud. The old road ran parallel to the steep hill and after twenty-five minutes of huffing and puffing, I finally made my way up there.

As I had assumed, Olivia was at the old balustrade. Her back to me, she looked out to sea. The barriers that lined the old road had never been up to much. It was like the council couldn't care less whether cars plunged off the edge of the cliff or not. It was said several cars had done exactly that, though it had been before we had been born. Rather than replace the old wooden balustrade with steel and concrete, the council had put up large neon signs with flashing amber lights. The signs were still there, their lights long since broken. My best friend was a dark shadow standing in between them, the yawning chasm of the bay below her.

'Olivia?' I was uneasy. She surely didn't mean to jump?

Olivia startled. As she turned towards me, I caught sight of her expression. Melancholy, yes; suicidal – no.

'What do you want?' She looked back at the bay, the swirling mass of waves below.

A good question. What did I want? To say sorry. But I'd already done that, back at the party. It hadn't meant anything.

'I just ...' I let the words hang between us. The breeze picked up, rustling through the trees. Suddenly the waves seemed much louder to my ears.

'You just ... *what?*'

Olivia turned around, her arms folded. She stayed next to the old broken-down balustrade, her feet on the wet earth.

I shrugged. 'I don't know what to say. I don't know what happened. I'm pathetic, I ...'

Self-pitying tears bubbled up within me. I hastily wiped one away, choked the rest down.

'... I shouldn't have lied to you.'

'No. You shouldn't have.' Olivia's tone was neutral, measured. It reminded me of Mum's when she told me off. Weird.

Silence, but for the waves and the breeze, settled between us again. Now what? I wasn't sure what to do next.

I had no coat on, just those stupid hot pants and vest top. I shivered as the light drizzle continued to fall on both of us. In moments we were more than drenched than if it had been pouring.

'This is stupid. Let's go back.' I placed my freezing hands under my armpits. 'We can talk about it, somewhere warm.'

Oliva flicked a hand at me. 'There's no point.'

Somehow, this was worse than when Olivia had been raging at me in The Grange. 'C'mon, Olivia. You're my best friend.'

'Was.'

Pain lanced through my chest. 'No, still. I let you down. I will make it up to you! I swear?'

Olivia hesitated. She looked to the bay again, speaking with her back to me, as if she couldn't bear to look at me.

'You were the one person I could trust, Jaz.'

Shame filled my veins. Olivia was right. I had been the only one in her corner, all these years: through school; her parents' arguments and their divorce; to college and beyond. Olivia had been miserable for years, sure there was something wrong with her if her own family couldn't be bothered with her. I had known all of this. Yet all it had taken was Ellie and her exotic promise to make me abandon my best friend.

'I know.' I conceded. 'I'm sorry.'

'You keep saying that.'

'It's because it's true!' My cry, louder than I meant it to be, echoed right across the bay. 'Please believe me?'

Olivia sighed. 'Just … go away, Jaz.'

I couldn't believe it. I stood there, in shock, unable to comprehend what was happening.

Our friendship was over.

''Bye.' I hoped the finality might make her regret her choice, turn around again. She didn't. Hot tears blurred my vision. A single sob wracked in my chest as I walked away from my best friend, back towards the headland pathway.

Later, I would wonder if those tears obscured my vision so much I had simply veered off the path … Or perhaps the soft, wet earth simply fell away beneath my boots? Maybe it was a combination of both.

Whatever happened, I felt a sudden and huge pull sideways, towards the edge of the cliff face. My feet went from under me. I windmilled my arms, tried to dig my boots into the mud, yet I could find only air.

I heard a scream. Olivia's face rushed towards me, but inexplicably I fell backwards and she was gone again. Seemingly in slow motion, branches and thorns tore into my flesh.

I was falling.

Sixteen

My back hit the ground at last.

There was a sickening crack as my thigh hit something; pain flashed through my body as quickly as electricity. For a moment, I was stunned. The air was knocked out of me so hard I struggled to draw another breath, my mind reeling. Stupefied, I lay there a moment, unable to comprehend what had just happened.

'Jaz! Do. Not. Move!'

I heard Olivia yell above, though I could not see her anymore. I attempted to raise my head. Shooting pain pierced through my skull, which seemed to awake agony in the rest of my body. My thighbone felt as if someone had injected it with fire. I shrieked with pain and horror. *Was it broken?* I tried to reach for my leg, as if that would make any difference.

A small shower of earth tumbled down. I heard feet scraping on granite and then Olivia was beside me. Her face stared down at mine, drawn and white, her eyes wide with shock.

'What the hell happened?' She demanded, as unsure as me what had just occurred.

'I don't know.' I winced. Just breathing hurt.

Despite the shock or maybe because of it, Olivia cracked

a wide smile. 'When I told you to piss off, I didn't expect you to jump, you silly cow!'

We both laughed … And then I groaned. *Jesus.*

'Can you sit up?' Olivia grabbed my shoulders.

With difficulty and through gritted teeth, I managed to. I realised where we were. Through blind luck, I had landed on a small stone shelf under the cliff pathway. I could see the Victorian railway across the bay, just metres away, cut into the rockface.

'What about standing?'

As I tried to shift and stand with my best friend, a wave of pain hit me so hard nausea washed through me. I dry-heaved, my head spinning. Olivia sat me down again.

'I'll call Dad.' She reached for her phone in her pocket. She groaned. It wasn't there. 'What about your bag?'

'I can't see it.' I gulped in deep breaths. 'Maybe it went over? … No, don't!'

Olivia immediately lay down on the shelf, making a grab for something. She turned back: 'I can see it, hanging off a bloody gorse.' Her expression was grim, 'Just out of reach! How typical is that?'

Again, we laughed. It was either that, or cry.

'I'll call the coastguard,' She said. 'There's the box!'

She was right, it wasn't far away. But then I remembered it was broken. I told Olivia.

'Give us a break!' She shouted at the grey sky, though whom exactly she was yelling at I had no clue. Olivia didn't believe in God, so maybe Mother Nature?

'You'll have to go down the path, get someone.'

Olivia looked down at me, torn. It was clear she did not want to leave me. I didn't want her to either, but what choice did we have? Mum was at work and thought I was at home.

Jim was drunk. It could be hours before anyone missed us and there was no guarantee they'd look up here, anyway.

'I can't, you're soaked. You'll get hypothermia before I make it back with anyone.' Olivia's gaze fell on the cliff railway. 'There's an intercom in there, remember?'

My pain-addled brain hadn't remembered. But with Olivia's words, I recalled using the cliff railway with her the previous summer, escorting some Spanish Tourists around Winby. The language school in Exmorton had paid us both twenty-five pounds, cheaper than a teacher. We'd been surprised to find our old teacher, Jenny Keller's Dad, operating the railway. He seemed more carefree than he ever had in school. He chatted with us amiably. Olivia was right ... there had been an intercom right next to the big levers that powered the cab. The railway system was an expensive piece of kit, so the intercom would be rigged to an alarm system. Except:

'The railway's locked.' I said, 'I saw it ... It's all chained up.'

'Jaz, I'm a policeman's daughter.' Olivia chastised. 'I'll figure it out.'

Olivia made her way across the rock shelf, back on to the pathway, disappearing out of sight. The wind picked up around me. I strained in the increasing darkness to see Olivia as she picked her way carefully across the headland. Without the stimulus of talking to her, black shapes started to jump out at me, swirling in the periphery of my vision. I knew I must not let them take over; I could slump and fall from the ledge. Even so, it seemed like a massive effort to keep my eyes open or keep my head up.

About ten agonising minutes later, an alarm blared through the night, casting the cliff with red warning lights, our own personal lighthouse.

'Reckon that'll get their attention down there?' Olivia slid back down on to the shelf with me, as if from nowhere.

'What did you do?' I imagined her unpicking those huge padlocks on the levers with a hairpin, a movie heroine crossed with a cat burglar.

Olivia shrugged and grinned 'Broke a window. Heritage site … Hardly going to be double-glazed, is it?'

Olivia put her arms around me, supporting my head and shoulders with her body. Finally, I was able to surrender to the darkness.

Seventeen

As I came round again, I discovered Olivia and I were no longer alone on the little rock shelf under the cliff pathway. The alarm had brought people running up to the top of the headland, shining torches on us. My Granfer and his friend Alec were also present. Alec was a farmer type who lived out at Linwood, the village up the road. He shared lifeboat duties with Granfer and half a dozen other Winby residents. It had been their weekly meeting at The Moon, they said.

'Lucky you fell tonight!' Granfer shouted.

I wanted to say I'd rather I hadn't fallen at all, but for some reason I couldn't summon up the words.

He sighed, stroking the hair out of my face. 'Your ma is gonna go nuts, maid. But happen she'll be glad to get you back.'

I blinked and I was lying on a gurney, covered by a foil survival blanket. Olivia had one wrapped round her too. Granfer had splinted my leg with a tree branch; it was still poking into my flesh. Two worried paramedics fussed around me, muttering about protocol. They told my ever-capable Granfer he should have waited, but he pretended he had no clue what they were talking about. As someone placed an oxygen mask over my face, I passed out again.

I awoke in hospital, stiff and thirsty, my leg suspended in traction. Mum's white drawn face peered at me, asking me how I felt.

Like crap, I croaked.

Mum smiled and said, 'Good, you nearly gave me a heart attack and put me in here as well, you little bugger.' Then she kissed me on the forehead.

Olivia was there every day at visiting time, bringing me her ipad so I could read and watch movies. I tried asking about that night, but every time Olivia refused to be drawn on it:

'You've got bigger things to worry about.' She gave me a wan smile, indicated my smashed leg.

Olivia wasn't wrong. I wanted to know when I could go home. Mum sighed and said she wasn't sure, batting away my enquiries about it 'just' being a broken leg. Because of her dodging the subject, I knew it wasn't just a broken leg at all; I realised it was going to make a big difference to my life. I was right.

I couldn't run anymore.

Mum and Olivia were in hospital with me when they told me. I wasn't stupid; I knew there could be a chance of it. All the same I had been hoping against hope a miracle might happen and my running would not be affected. But as soon as the specialist came in, that look on his face, I knew what he would say before the words came out of his mouth.

Mum and Olivia looked on the bright side, saying I'd prove everyone wrong, but I knew I wouldn't. After all the operations, I would be left with a limp, the specialist said. There was no way I could qualify for county level running with that. Hopelessness crashed in on me: running was all I'd ever been any good at. Now what would I do with my life?

Olivia smiled. 'You'll do whatever you want to do.'

I hoped she was right.

~

Days became two weeks and suddenly summer was over. College began again. I was still in hospital in Exmorton, so Olivia brought in books and homework. She read to me and told me everything that had been going on at college, so I wouldn't feel left out or get left behind. Ellie had since gone back to London but sent a huge, expensive bouquet, unable to face coming into the hospital. I had not seen Niall since before the party, though he'd tagged a picture of me and him on Instagram with the message, *You'll be okay. N X.* I initially felt let down by such a seemingly superficial message, but as time went on I realised the truth of his words.

I *would* be okay. Because I had Olivia.

After two operations, five metal pins and a lot of gruelling physiotherapy, I was finally able to go home. Life in hospital was so small, even Winby felt big. I wasn't allowed to mope about, either. Mum was ceaselessly cheerful, telling me life would be back on track before I knew it, no matter whether I could run or not. On crutches, I was still expected to help out with housework or errands however I could and I loved her for that.

No longer the slug-a-bed she used to be, it was Olivia who arrived every morning bright and early, pulling me from mine instead as I resisted.

'Come on you!' Olivia trilled, 'We're going out.'

'Where?' I said shoved a pillow over my head, only for Olivia to grab it off me seconds later.

'I don't know, do I.' Olivia said simply. 'Out and about. Come on!'

We found ourselves back down at the seafront. As we walked towards Teddy's, we noted The Grange stood empty again, a large FOR SALE sign outside. So, The Mackintoshes would not be back. Neither of us said anything, but it seemed right, as if that chapter of our lives was over.

Inside, Teddy's looked as it always did: that faded, ridiculous mural; the dingy café curtains; those cheap tables and chairs. Behind the café counter, yet another new clueless counter assistant struggled to keep up with demand as the ever-temperamental coffee machine bust a gasket and erupted with steam.

'It's okay!' The girl in front of us said. 'I'll take it without foam. Even though it *is* a cappuccino.'

I recognised that voice. The girl in front turned around and grinned at me and Olivia, her face covered in glitter. Yep, it was Jenny Keller again.

'Jasmine!' She shrieked, looking for her purse in her voluminous hippy bag, 'I haven't seen you in ages! Omigod I heard what happened. No way! Olivia said you just got out of hospital. Were there any fit male nurses in there?'

The counter assistant coughed conspicuously, holding his hand out for her money. Realising Jenny was still searching for her purse, I laughed and proffered a note instead.

'I'll get this.' I said …

Double Tap

'It's always too late for sorries.'
Neil Gaiman

Eighteen

Saturday, August 25th

… The bell tinkled above the door, just as our drinks were set down on the counter. One hot chocolate with cream and sprinkles for Olivia, just a tea for me. *A guilt buy*, my treacherous brain insisted, but I pushed the thought back down. Next to it, a cappuccino. *Who was that for?*

'Thanks so much, I'll shout you next time.' Jenny Keller squeezed my shoulder.

I forced a smile, hoping my confusion did show on my face. Olivia seemed oblivious, dipping one finger into the cream floating on top of her drink as she picked it up. I was distracted again. Behind us, the door stood open: whomever had come was loitering on the threshold, looking at his phone. A curtain of hair obscured his face.

'Four eighty.' The wan guy behind the counter's name badge read RAY, which seemed completely at odds with his moody expression. Underneath his name was 'service with a smile!' but apparently he'd never read his own badge. I handed a five pound note over, not waiting for the change. He proffered it anyway as we all turned away from the counter.

'Keep it.'

'Cheers.' Ray rolled his eyes at the silver twenty pence piece: such riches. He dropped it in the charity box next to the till.

I moved with the other two towards a table. Olivia was already sitting down, scrolling through her phone and double-tapping the screen. Jenny seemed to think she was joining us. I wasn't against it, it was just weird. But maybe Olivia had invited her. Or maybe Jenny had invited herself. She wasn't backwards at coming forwards.

Then something even weirder happened. Jenny froze where she was as the door to the café closed. Her eyes locked with the guy's who had just come in. Tall, good-looking, self-assured: Nat Williams. I knew him immediately, even though I'd never talked to him in my life. Jenny had gone out with him, in the first year of college ... Until he'd cheated on her.

With Olivia.

Nat pocketed his phone. He looked Jenny up and down, a derisive smile on his face. 'Jenny ... Olivia.'

Jenny did not reply. 'Actually, you have this.'

She shoved the cappuccino towards me. I took it without a word. Jenny adjusted her bag strap and swept out of Teddy's. The door closed behind her, that little bell tinkling after her like a child's toy.

Nat gave us a wolfish grin and raised his eyebrows at Olivia. 'Awww. Something I said?'

'Piss off, Nat.' Oliva barely looked up from her phone, as if he bored her.

Nat laughed and moved towards the counter. As we sat down, confusion clouded my brain a second time. Jenny and Olivia didn't speak because of Nat. None of us were friends. Why had we been about to sit down together? What had just happened? It felt significant, but I wasn't sure why.

'I thought Jenny hated you?' The words come, unbid my lips. 'For breaking her and Nat up last year?'

Olivia's expression darkened. 'Oh, is that what happened?'

I hesitated. It had been a while ago, plus I hadn't even been at the party Olivia and Nat had got together. Jenny hadn't been there either, which was why Nat had been able to cheat with Olivia. Well, that was what boys did, when their girlfriends were out of the picture, wasn't it? It was one of the reasons I had to go to Ellie's party, to keep an eye on Niall.

'Wow.' Olivia took in my silence, dumping her phone on the table at last. 'So, you *do* think I went behind Jenny's back! How long have you thought this?'

It wasn't my fault. Olivia honed in on other people's boyfriends, flirting and tossing her hair in what she thought was a seductive manner. Since we'd started sixth form college, Olivia had become The Good Time Girl. She was more interested in partying than studying. She let got behind on all her work. But worse than that, she'd the one other girls were automatically suspicious of: *The Slutty One.* She never shared with me any details of other girls' boyfriends she'd poached, but she must have. There was no smoke without fire … Right?

'Don't you get it? You're getting a *reputation*.' I cast my eyes downwards at my shoes.

Olivia stared into her hot chocolate mug. 'I would never have thought you were the type to worry about reputations.'

'You purposefully go after other girl's boyfriends!' I

said, 'It's not right.'

'And what about the boyfriends?' Olivia replied, 'Do they have reputations? Or is it all just 'Evil Olivia' who bewitches them?'

I sigh. Ellie's face from that morning flashed back into my brain. She had presented me with a plausible case. 'You *know* why Olivia can't come. She'll drink too much and get between couples like some overgrown gooseberry. It's embarrassing for everyone, including her. Trust me, I'm actually thinking of Olivia in the long run.'

I held up both hands. 'Forget I said anything, okay?'

There was an uncomfortable pause. Olivia glared at me with shiny eyes. She muttered something I could not catch. Then she pushed the half full cup towards me and rose from the table, anger crackling through her movements. Remorse flooded through me. I grabbed her hand before she could sweep out of Teddy's like Jenny had, just ten minutes before.

'Look. There's a party at Ellie's, tonight …' I began.

' … So?'

'… She doesn't want you to come.' I forced it out in one breath.

There: I said it. Olivia would realise I wasn't behind her exclusion and we could move on.

'You and Ellie don't even get on,' I pointed out, 'no biggie, right?'

Olivia's eyes bulged. 'Wait a minute … You're still going?'

Guilt hit me full on. Yet still I tried to shake it off. 'I have to. Becky Jarvis is going, too. She's made it clear she wants Niall!'

A strange, bitter smile curled Olivia's lip. '*Of course* you would think that. Well, I guess you have 'no choice'. Go guard your man from the evil sluts.'

Olivia's sarcasm felt deafening. I thought she would be angry about being excluded; maybe even angry with me for still going. But I didn't recognise this reaction. I felt out of my depth, like I was seeing a hidden, raw part of Olivia, but I didn't know why.

I grabbed for her hand. 'You don't mind, do you?'

Olivia wrenched it away. She leant down, hissed in my ear. 'Oh, I don't mind. Ellie is nothing to me. She can have a party every frigging night and invite the sodding Dobre Brothers for all I care. But you? I thought you were better than … *this*.'

My brain struggled to process what she was saying. 'Then I won't go?'

'For God's sake, Jaz!' Olivia brought the heels of her hands to her eyes, to stop tears from spilling over. 'It's not about the party, you idiot.'

Stunned, I watched Olivia stalk out the same way as Jenny, followed by the tinkling of that stupid bell above the door.

Nineteen

I waited in Teddy's for another twenty minutes, sure Olivia would come back. She'd overreacted about stuff before, flouncing off in a huff. Within half an hour, she'd always reappeared or called me, rolling her eyes and laughing about it. *Time of the month twenty-four-seven*, she'd grin, doing air quotes with both fingers. That's what her Dad always said. Ugh, parents.

When it became clear Olivia would not be returning, I gave up and trudged back to the flat. It was only three hours until the party; I had to get ready. I'd already planned my outfit multiple times, pairing various tops and jeans or skirts, over and over. Ellie had stuck her head in my wardrobe, digging out a powder blue vest top, denim skirt and blue shrug with flip flops and one of her necklaces. It still didn't seem 'right'. Probably because she'd stood over me as I'd bought a matching blue lingerie set in town two days' earlier.

'You want to look great on every layer, just in case.' Ellie raised an eyebrow at me, smiling.

Unease blossomed in my stomach. I knew what Ellie was referring to. As far as she was concerned, I was the odd one out: the 'pure' one, the naïve one, the one who 'needed' to have her 'cherry' popped … whether I wanted to or not.

'You *have* been going out nearly four weeks.' Ellie pointed out. 'You should go for it, the night of the party. It's perfect.'

I regarded the lingerie, morose. 'I dunno though … I'm not sure I'm ready?'

'Oh God, no one's 'ready'!' Ellie raised her eyes sky-wards, 'The first time is always crap for girls. You just get on with it. You'll be glad you got it over with when it's done. Trust me.'

'He's your brother, what do you care?' I muttered.

Ellie's nostrils flared. 'I'm just looking out for you, Jaz. God! Don't you want to look nice?'

Don't you want to lose your virginity?, should have been the question. If I was being honest for once, the answer would have been, 'No!' It all seemed like such a hassle. I liked Niall, but in a few weeks he'd be back in London at university. I was realistic: he wouldn't have time for me, a second year college student back in the sticks. And if I was honest, would I have time for him? I had so many plans, I didn't want anything to put them in jeopardy. Sex seemed a big deal, fraught with potential problems. Better just to opt out altogether.

I couldn't say any of this to Ellie, of course. I'd confided in Olivia as always, showing her the blue matching lingerie set Ellie had made me buy.

Olivia wrinkled her nose, fingering the silky material. 'Not really you, is it?'

'It's not tarty.' I retorted, defensive.

'It doesn't matter what it is,' Olivia chose her words carefully, 'if it's not what you want?'

'Niall's nice.'

'… But?' Olivia challenged.

'No, he is. Niall's not the problem, it's just …'

I sighed. What was it, exactly? The weight of the expectation? The fear of being the 'odd one out'? Of disappointing Ellie?

'Talk to him.' Olivia said. 'You shouldn't have to go along with anything you don't want. I don't think he'd want you to either. But he can only know that if you talk about it first.'

But I hadn't talked to Niall. I'd gone out for coffees with him, walks on the beach, but the subject hadn't come up. But that must be what he wanted from me. All the magazines, the talk shows, the YouTube channels said men loved sex and expected it from girls. Ellie was more experienced than me, so I should just take her word for it. It couldn't be that big a deal.

I pushed these thoughts out of my mind as I got ready. After applying make-up and dressing in the outfit Ellie had chosen (including *that* lingerie set), my stomach was in knots. I looked at my reflection in my mirror. It was now or never. Before I could lose my nerve, I pushed my bedroom door open into the kitchen.

'So. Let's have a look at you.'

I turned to find Mum seated at the kitchen table. She wasn't supposed to be home from work yet. She usually came home for a bite to eat, then rushed off to her second job, cleaning at the caravan park. I had banked on writing her a quick note, perhaps even managing an extra hour or two past curfew, as Mum usually crashed out, exhausted. A blanket around her shoulders, she looked pale and drawn.

'I had a migraine, so knocked off early.' Mum flashed me

with a sardonic grin, knowing full well what my plan had been. 'You look nice.'

'Thanks.' I blotted my damp palms on my denim skirt. But I only felt nervous because Mum had pre-busted me about staying out late … *Right?*

She nodded at the necklace. 'That new?'

'No.' My mouth felt dry. 'It's Ellie's. The new girl who lives at The Grange?'

Mum's expression was impassive. 'Right. I've seen her go past the shop.'

She'd been unusually quiet and tired this summer. But if anything had happened, Mum wasn't telling me about it. As usual. I'd offered to help out, get a job for the summer to bring some extra money in, but she believed 'kids should be kids'. She said running the house was her problem, not mine. But it made me feel like a burden.

Mum's voice cut into my thoughts. 'I haven't seen Olivia for a while. Everything okay with you two?'

'Yeah, 'course.' I replied, a little too brightly.

'And are *you* all right, Jaz?'

I cursed inwardly. It was as if Mum had some kind of truth-seeking missile, hitting me straight in the conscience every time. How did she know? Was the expectation placed on me by Ellie about tonight so heavy she could feel it, too?

'I'm fine.' I lied.

Mum pursed her lips, disbelieving. I thought for a moment she was going to say I couldn't go. A flurry of complaints rose in my mouth in readiness … Yet, a small part of me also felt relief at the prospect of being banned.

Mum sighed. 'Okay. Have a nice time.'

I got out of the flat before she could change her mind, or grill me some more. Walking down to The Grange, a flurry of butterflies in my stomach took flight. Guilt followed: *What was Olivia doing, right now?*

I looked to my phone's blank screen. All I needed to do was press her name, she and I could be talking in an instant. I could be at her house in less than five minutes! We could fire up Netflix, open a bag of bacon crisps and a bottle of vodka. It would be like old times. Before college and everything started to get weird.

Best of all, I wouldn't have to worry about Niall, about Becky Jarvis, or even about Ellie. She might get mad at me, but it wouldn't last long. Ellie and Niall and the rest of the family would be back in London in less than three weeks. Olivia and I could start the second year at college, best friends again, everything back to normal.

Yet my disloyal feet kept walking towards the seafront.

Twenty

Music pumped from the house and out on the balcony of The Grange. On the patio, the sun and incoming tide behind a selection of teens holding beer bottles and wine glasses. As I drew closer, I could pick out their faces. I only recognised two from the year above me at college; the others I didn't know at all. Four girls in expensive dresses and sunglasses laughed too loud. They were hoping to attract the attention of three guys in badly-ironed shirts who were only pretending *not* to notice them. What was I doing? This was a waste of time. I turned on my heel, determined to go home after all.

'Jaz!' Ellie appeared out of the patio windows, holding a tray of tapas.

Too late. I turned and gave her my breeziest, 'I'm-not-out-of-my-depth' smile.

'Come on up!' She trilled.

The front door was on the latch as I let myself in. Teens congregated in the hall and every single room. Ellie must have invited the whole of Winby and most of Exmorton too (apart from Olivia). I dodged past couples and groups everywhere. I nodded the occasional 'Hello' to people I thought I recognised, though no one invited me to join them. Was

I supposed to just go up to people and chat? I had no idea. How did everyone else handle this? I didn't want to be a tag-along, but I was also aware I might seem standoffish. God, why was this so hard!

Then Andrew Franklin, Jenny Keller's boyfriend, snaked an arm out and grabbed me. His face was already flushed and merry from alcohol.

'Hi … you?' He yelled above the music. Deflated, I realised he could not remember my name. '… Where's Olivia?'

'Oh, she … um … couldn't come.' I felt the tinge of embarrassment in my cheeks and prayed they were not flaming red.

Andrew shrugged. 'Oh, shame.'

'Hi, Jaz!'

Jenny appeared next to Andrew. She looked like she'd walked straight out of nineteen ninety-six: Union Jack dress over flared trousers, looped beads around her neck. Andrew put his arm around her shoulders. I envied the easy way they were together. I had never felt relaxed around Niall. I was always wondering when he would realise how boring I was, how inexperienced. How I was not worth bothering with.

'Olivia here yet?' Jenny took a slug of wine from a coffee mug.

That question again. Before I could answer, the music stopped. There was a hubbub of voices, then I heard someone was berated for standing on the plug and pulling it from the wall. Distracted, Andrew and Jenny turned away from me and were re-absorbed back into the throng. Phew.

I continue to pick my way around people. I finally made it to the patio doors, then out onto the balcony. Ellie was deep in conversation with another girl I did not recognise.

She was painfully thin and wearing postmodern-style paint-splashed denims, with her hair piled up on her head as if she were going to a debutante ball. If Ellie saw me, she gave no indication of it. I stood nearby, smiling awkwardly, hoping to catch her eye. A minute or two passed with no luck.

'Hey.' I reached forward and tugged on Ellie's dress, like a child trying to get the attention of her otherwise-occupied mother.

Ellie smiled and swooped on me. She kissed both my cheeks, as if she had only just noticed me.

'Darling!' She'd never addressed me as such before. She indicated her denim-clad friend. 'This is Victoria, she's down from London for the weekend. Vic, this is Jasmine.'

'Oh, the runner.' Victoria offered one bony hand to me to shake. 'Ellie says you're the only one worth knowing in this backwater.'

'We like it.' As I said the words, I wondered who 'we' were. Certainly not Ellie, who made her disdain for Winby clear every chance she got. Me and Olivia, perhaps … But was there even a 'Me and Olivia' anymore?

'Jasmine's Niall's girlfriend.' Ellie said with sly eyes at Victoria. She grinned at me, by way of explanation: 'Victoria and Niall used to go out.'

Uncomfortable prickles broke out over my arms at the mention of this. Victoria, however, took this in her stride.

'Hardly 'going out', Ellie.' She drawled, 'We just hooked up once in a while, nothing serious.'

'Hooked up'? What did that even mean! Dumbstruck I nodded, hoping my silence would be taken as cool indifference.

'Jasmine wants to study in London.' Ellie told Victoria.

'Oh, you don't study in London …' Victoria smirked.

' ... You live the lifestyle, right.' I cut in.

All of a sudden, it was too much. I wanted out. Ellie's glare bored into me. I knew she thought I was being rude, but I didn't care. What the hell was I doing here? I cast my gaze back into the living room. There was Niall, standing by the fridge, a beer bottle in hand.

Becky Jarvis was making a beeline straight for him.

'Oh look, there's Niall, back in a sec.' I declared, not meaning it. I left both girls in my wake.

I had to get between Becky and Niall.

Twenty-One

Closer and without a bunch of people in the way, Becky of course made it to Niall before I did. Hemmed in by the fridge, the countertop and two partygoers making out, Niall had nowhere to go. Becky took full advantage of this, leaning on the countertop so Niall had no choice but stay where he was, or risk brushing his body against hers.

I'd seen Olivia employ this technique to good effect, before. Would Becky be able to steal Niall, right from under my nose? I called out to him, but my words were snatched by the music. *Damn it.* Then another laughing girl got in my way, that coffee mug still hand.

Jenny Keller again.

'Hi.' I swallowed my irritation down, attempting to peer over her shoulder.

I didn't have time for Jenny right now. From nowhere Andrew Franklin leapt in front of me, attempting to kiss her cheek, but drunkenly planting one on her ear instead. Jenny thought this was hysterical and went off into peals of tipsy laughter. I made a move, trying to squeeze past them, but Jenny grabbed my arm.

'So, is Olivia coming later, then?'

'No.' I replied, annoyed. What was this obsession with

Olivia? I could see Niall was still hemmed in by Becky at the fridge.

'I just wanted to tell her thanks.'

'What for?' I replied, my interest piqued, tearing my gaze away from Niall and Becky at last.

'For Nat.' Jenny said. 'She did me a favour!'

'Right.'

I was distracted all over again by Becky and Niall. Becky had edged even closer. Niall was practically against the kitchen wall. Jenny and Andrew, hand in hand now, finally got out my way. I stalked into the kitchen, face like thunder.

'Jaz!' Was that guilt in Niall's eyes ... or relief? As ever, I couldn't tell.

Becky jumped like a child caught doing something she shouldn't. She flashed me her best innocent smile. 'Hey, we were just talking about you.'

'I've been looking for you.' I said to Niall, ignoring Becky.

Niall nodded. 'Yeah, let's go somewhere, shall we?'

Becky pouted, put out, watching us disappear out onto the terrace. As we made our way towards the sea wall, I felt a kind of childish triumph: Becky had failed, I had stopped her!

Niall sat down, watching the tide coming in below. I sat next to him, edging closer, rehearsing the expected event of the night in my mind's eye. Niall was a nice guy. Perhaps Ellie was right; the first time was crap for girls, I might as well get it over with? I was tired of being a tag-along, the outside, the naïve one.

'This isn't working.'

I was so busy thinking of what might happen, Niall's actual words seemed to come out of nowhere. I regarded him, slack-jawed.

'I'm going back to London on Monday.' Niall explained, 'I've got loads on with uni… Long distance relationships don't work. I think we should break up.'

A pang coursed through me, though I wasn't sure what it was: rejection? Pain? Or irritation I didn't get there first?

'Fine.' I bluffed. 'I was thinking the same.'

'Oh.' Niall blinked. He'd clearly been expecting more of a scene. 'That's good, then.'

Then he was hugging me. He got up from the sea wall, indicating his empty beer bottle: he was going to get another.

He stopped at the patio door 'It's been fun, Jaz.'

'Yeah.' I said in a flat voice.

Niall went inside again.

I was surprised to realise I was not upset. Niall and I had never really got off the ground. I hadn't allowed it to. I'd always done what I thought was expected of me, trying to be 'cool', thinking that would make me interesting. I'd always held back, worried he would think the 'real' me boring. But that had made me boring, so Niall had broken up with me!

I felt a chuckle rise in my throat: it was actually quite funny. I had to tell Olivia.

'I thought you were better than *this*.'

As Olivia's words from that afternoon boomeranged back to me, I joined the dots at last. With all my talk of 'reputations', I'd judged Olivia and let her down. I'd never asked her what really happened between her and Nat. Plus Jenny didn't seem to have any lasting hatred towards my best friend. So what the hell had I been thinking?

Sitting on the sea wall, I looked at the party going on around me. Everywhere couples and groups of friends were laughing, drinking and dancing. I was alone. Without Olivia, I was nothing. *That* was why Jenny and Andrew had been asking where she was. Olivia and I came as a package. I needed to get out of there and go beg her forgiveness, right now. I had been a crap friend.

As I attempted to leave, through the throngs of people, Becky popped up again. 'So … You and Niall?'

I glanced across the patio to my now-ex-boyfriend. I'd thought it was all so inevitable. As if Becky Jarvis could magically steal Niall away from me! He was chatting with another lad, next to the patio doors, his face lit up laughing. I felt nothing for him.

'You're welcome to him.' I told Becky.

I slipped away from the party, without looking back.

Twenty-Two

At Olivia's, I rang the doorbell and waited. Nothing. Jim's car was missing from the driveway, he must be at work. I took my phone out from my pocket and pressed Olivia's name.

But her phone rang and rang. Then voicemail kicked in: *'Hi, this is Olivia's phone, leave a message, byeeeeeeeeee!'*

I was not sure why, but listening to that cheery message, I was struck by a sense of foreboding. The house seemed empty, the windows were dark. I knew Olivia had to be home. Everyone else we knew had been at the party at The Grange. It was possible she was asleep or watching Netflix with the sound turned up in her bedroom on the other side of the house.

I decided to let myself in. I had lots of times before. I knew where Jim kept the spare key: under a large planter of pansies to the side of the property. For a police officer, he was surprisingly lax about security.

I fit it in the lock and turned it, disappearing inside.

Later, there would be gaps in my memory of what happened next. Momentary flashes would return to me. The television in Olivia's room, streaming a Disney movie, its music score ridiculously jaunty. My shaking hands, trying to call 999. The ambulance, its blue light standing idle in the darkness. The green coats of the paramedics, their quiet voices. My mother's taut, white face, her arm clamped around me, holding me up. Granfer standing on the sidelines, seemingly speechless, not knowing what to do.

Worst of all: Olivia's slack, dead legs. Dangling from the shower cubicle in her en-suite bathroom, where she had hanged herself with a dressing gown cord.

Twenty-Three

The next few days passed in what felt like slow motion. I kept expecting my phone to ring, Olivia's breezy voice on the other end, '*So what's the plan?*' Instead there was only silence.

I went online, searching through Olivia's social media profiles, just to see pictures of her. I didn't go online much; I didn't see the point. I had an Instagram account, but I barely updated it. I was surprised by the number of sites Olivia had. Instagram, Pinterest, Snapchat, Reddit, Tumblr, Quora, Facebook, Twitter – she'd signed up to all of them. As I scrolled through, I discovered there were lots of new posts for Olivia, though she would never read them. Though the posts were all expressed differently, each one could be summed up in two words:

I'm sorry.

At first, I thought the posts meant they were sorry Olivia had killed herself. But as I kept scrolling, I began to see others. These were ones that had come earlier in the summer and even before that, before Olivia's suicide. Supposed 'jokes' became sarky messages, which in turn became ones that were blatantly abusive.

Olivia had been trolled and cyber-bullied for months.

As I catalogued them in my horrified brain, I noticed the posts followed two themes: Olivia was a slut, or she was fat. Sometimes the posts contained both. There were memes too, including photo-shopped images of Olivia's head with accusative cartoon letters. Most of the worst posts and images were anonymous. Even so, it was obvious the messages had stepped up in number and intensity after Ellie had moved to The Grange.

Weirdly, Olivia had 'liked' all the shitty, bullying posts. I cast my mind back to the day of the party: Olivia had been in Teddy's, double-tapping the screen of her phone, one post after another. Was this her way of hollering back, saying she wasn't bothered by the abuse? That certainly seemed Olivia's logic.

But why hadn't she told me? I sighed, holding my head in my hands. Because I had been a crap friend, that was why. The posts had started when we'd begun college, which was when I had started drawing away from Olivia. That was before Ellie was even on the scene. By the time she'd arrived in Winby, I'd begun my quest to reinvent myself. I'd told Olivia to 'just ignore' Ellie, over and over. It's not about the party you *idiot*, were Olivia's last words to me.

Why hadn't I realised sooner?

~

Olivia's funeral was small. Both her parents were there. They managed not to argue for once. Natalie, Olivia's sister was there too. Also present were Olivia's grandparents on her mother's side; then Mum, me, Granfer and a small selection of people from college, including Andrew Franklin and Jenny Keller. Ellie was unable to face coming but had sent a huge bouquet of flowers in the shape of a heart.

Looking at the arrangements my mother murmured, 'Oh isn't that nice?'

Like the coward I was, I'd nodded. Really I wanted to grab the arrangement and shred it to pieces. Ellie might be sorry now, but she was a hypocrite. So was I.

'It's not your fault, maid.' Granfer had said that morning, knotting his tie. He'd last worn his suit for Mum's wedding to my Dad, nearly twenty years ago.

I knew Granfer's words were not true, though. I'd had the chance to stand up for Olivia. But like everyone else in her life, I had let her down when it counted. I was the one person who was supposed to stand by her, no matter what. I hadn't been there for Olivia, I had totally let her down. I stood in the cemetery for my best friend, with Mum and Granfer. We watched the coffin go in, laden with flowers. I felt numb.

Jim had a small wake back at the house. Mum escorted me back there, knowing I didn't want to go there again, yet wordlessly encouraging me to face my fear. Some sandwiches and cake were offered on a table against one wall. On the other, a computer had been rigged up, showing a slideshow of pictures of Olivia. In all, she was smiling, yet I noticed too late the sadness in her eyes in every single one.

'She was a good girl.' Jim said, over and over as people expressed their condolences.

I wanted to scream, 'How would you know?' Jim had barely noticed his eldest daughter, no matter what she did, good or not! Olivia's mother Polly dabbed her eyes, nodding whenever someone said how sorry they were. But were Jim and Polly really sorry? They had been bad parents, caught up in their own lives. Natalie sat alone under the stairs of her old home, amongst the coats. Some of the coats were Olivia's, still hanging on the peg where she left them.

I wanted to say something to Natalie, tell her it was all my fault. I was the final straw that made Olivia feel life was not worth living anymore. Yet whenever I opened my mouth to speak, no sound came out.

As minute by agonising minute passed, people started to talk about other things: the proof life moves on. I took my chance. I crept out of the front room, towards the front door and out into the street. I was wearing a black skirt, white shirt and my old school shoes because I didn't have a black dress suitable for a funeral, I didn't expect to have to go to one at my age. Even so, I found myself running towards the seafront. I hadn't warmed up, so within my minutes my chest felt tight and my old ankle injury started to twinge, but still I pushed on.

I saw there was activity at The Grange as I made it on to the seafront. Suitcases were piled up outside the front door and the car stood next to the building, its boot raised in readiness. Ellie and her parents were moving out, going back to London. Ste and Niall had gone already, the day after the party.

Ellie was standing at the sea wall. She was wearing that red dress from the day Olivia and I met her. How long ago that seemed! I slowed as I reached the sea wall, looking up at Ellie above. She snapped back to attention as she noticed me, shrinking away. I stared back, the one with the upper hand for once, as if we'd traded places.

'Jasmine.' She said quietly. 'How was it?'

I folded my arms. 'Like you'd expect.'

I wanted her to say she was sorry for her part in what happened. Instead, Ellie just averted her eyes, plucking at the hem of her dress like a little girl.

I sigh. 'I know … About the trolling?'

Ellie's eyes widened in horror. She looked for a moment as if she was going to deny it, then appeared to change her mind.

'It wasn't meant to be serious.' Ellie whispered. 'I didn't think …'

'No, you didn't.'

Nor did I, I wanted to add.

'I thought she liked arguing … If she didn't, why didn't she just block us?' Ellie stopped herself. Closed her eyes. 'I'm sorry.'

Maybe she wanted me to forgive her, say it was okay now, or things would get better? But it wasn't my place. That was Olivia's, but she was gone now.

Forever.

Leaving Ellie on the balcony, I started running again. I ran across the shale as fast as I could in sensible shoes. On The Moon pub steps a man, drinking far too early, whooped as I raced past. I faltered, slipping on the algae-covered rocks and falling to my knees. Normally this would have embarrassed me, but this time I just didn't care.

Ellie had at least been consistent. She'd never liked Olivia and had no problem letting her know where she stood. Me? I'd pretended to be on Olivia's side and then abandoned her the first chance I got. Mine was the worse crime, no question.

I thought of the last time I had run across the beach, just days before. I'd had gone home and showered, then I'd met Olivia at Teddy's. I'd let her know I thought she was a slut, then told her how Ellie didn't want her to go to the party, but I was still going. Why?

I was a jealous person.

Going to the party was never about Niall! It was about putting Olivia in her place. I wanted to prove I was 'somebody' without her. That was why I had gravitated towards Ellie … I wanted to feel important. I'd made that toxic belief the priority, instead of my best friend.

What felt like seconds later, I was back at home, with no memory of having travelled there. My shoes were wet through. I'd trodden shale and seawater throughout the flat. My mind in turmoil, I found myself wandering around the living room, around and around. I felt a sob rise in my throat and choked it down.

When did it start? When did I become jealous of Olivia? A few weeks ago? A few years? Or was it there, from the start? Had I just been waiting, all this time, for an opportunity to betray her?

'Jaz? Jasmine!'

The front door slammed, my mother's voice sounding through ahead of her. I didn't answer.

'There you are.' Mum appeared in the living room, her face a picture of concern. Granfer trailed behind her. 'I didn't see you leave the funeral … Where have you been?'

I opened my mouth to answer, but that sob escaped. All the tears I'd been putting off poured forth, a flash flood. Shoulders wracked, I leant forward as if someone had punched me in the gut. The pain was physical.

Mum rushed forwards and held on to me before I fell to me knees. She smoothed my hair just like she did when I was a little girl, yet she couldn't make this better. Still she attempted soothing noises, saying 'I know… I know…' over and over. Maybe she *did* know what it was like to let someone down so spectacularly and have to live with it for the rest of her life? I was reminded of how much I didn't know about her, about life, about myself.

Finally, after what seemed like hours, I had nothing left: I felt physically and emotionally drained. Mum helped me out of my wet clothes, putting me to bed like I was a small child again.

Exhausted, I fell into an uneasy sleep where I dreamt of Olivia. We were back at school. She was ahead of me in the corridor. No matter how much I ran to catch up, she would turn the corner, just out of sight. I awoke to birds singing outside the window, only for the knowledge Olivia was gone to hit me all over again. I knew what my dream meant. I could never make this right with Olivia. It was too late. I had to live with it, somehow.

But how?

Twenty-Four

'We're going out.'

I looked up from the breakfast table. Mum's face lined with concern. Granfer appeared in the kitchen area, holding his shoes. In the past week or so, he had taken to sleeping over on the sofa most nights. 'Just in case', I heard Mum say. But just in case of what? The worst had happened. Olivia was gone.

'I don't want to go anywhere.' I crushed dry cereal under a spoon on the table. Mum made no move to stop me, like she would normally.

'I've got the day off. You're coming.' Mum took a bit of toast.

I looked to Granfer to back me up. I could usually count on his support. But today, he shook his head. 'Do what your mother says, Jaz.'

It was the last blast of British Summertime. The August morning was grey and breezy, ahead of the Bank Holiday weekend. In just a few days I would be back at college, without Olivia. People would wonder where she was. I would have to say it, over and over. *Oh God.*

'I can't go out.' An edge of panic crept into my voice.

Mum pursed her lips. 'You can't stay in this flat forever.

You have to move forward. Little steps first.'

Each word felt like a dagger in my heart. Anger was never far away, now. 'And leave Olivia behind? You want to make me forget her?'

But Mum was not fazed. 'You will never forget her, darling. I wouldn't want you to. But you can't stay still. Do you think that is what Olivia wants?'

'Olivia is dead.' The words felt like lead on my tongue.

Mum helped me on with my coat. 'Yes, sweetheart. She is. And you have to keep on living.'

So, I trailed after her, all my objections failing to stir her. I realised where we were going when we'd trekked halfway up The Mount. The cemetery was on top of the Hill, just past the swan and its award-winning WELCOME TO WINBY floral arrangement. We'd come there just two weeks before, to put Olivia in the ground. Small groups of our college friends had stood around the grave, faces white, uncertain of what to say or do. So young, we weren't used to being in the presence of death. I'd hung back in the crowd, unwilling to see the coffin go in, hardly bearing the sound of earth striking the wooden top as first Jim and then Polly had thrown soil in, after my best friend.

The grave was pristine. Mum fussed around it anyway, clearing away the wilting and browned floral tributes on top (including Ellie's expensive heart). She had stopped halfway up the Mount to pick some wild flowers, which she placed in a small jam jar that acted as a vase.

'We could plant some flowers on the grave, for spring?' Mum looked back at me. I saw her eyes were shiny with tears. She hated this too, but none of us had any choice.

Even so, that familiar anger coursed through me. 'What's the point of flowers? Olivia's fucking dead, Mum!'

Mum flinched at my raised voice; shame quickly followed my rage. I cast my eyes downwards, from my mother's drawn face. It felt hard to breathe. How was I going to cope, without Olivia? I had no idea.

I walked forward, running my hand across the top of the headstone. Jim and Polly had spared no expense: it was shiny, polished marble, with gold lettering: OLIVIA JOY MARTIN. Inscribed underneath, her birth and death date, plus a short epitaph: *Always loved ... Never forgotten ... Forever missed.*

I would always miss Olivia; that much was true. I had loved her, but I had forgotten her. Why had I pulled away from her, let her down so badly? Why had I placed being popular like Ellie ahead of my best friend in the whole world?

I couldn't answer.

I looked back to the mound of Earth. Mum was no longer there, tending to the flowers. I looked behind me. There was Mum, forty or fifty feet away. She smiled and nodded at me: *Go on.*

I looked back to the gravesite and sighed. What did I say? I felt like if I started talking, I might never stop. Did I explain myself? Did I tell Olivia I had been jealous of her, of always walking in her shadow? I might have been known as 'the sporty one', but no one ever asked where I was! I was nobody without Olivia.

Olivia had always been the fun one, the memorable one. Olivia was larger than life, she was *somebody* all on her own. The tragedy was, she hadn't even known this. She was too filled with self-loathing, sure she couldn't be worth anyone's trouble. This was because everyone around her – her parents, people at school and college, ME – kept letting her down. I had failed her in the worst way possible and so hard everyone else. Not just for one night, but for years.

I remembered all the messages online, from the trolls. I leant down, resting my forehead against the cold marble. I closed my eyes, feeling the sting of tears there.

'I'm sorry.'

What else was there to say?

Rejoining Mum, she looked at me as if to say, *Okay?* I didn't feel any different. I still felt hollowed out, numb. Walking into town, I catalogued each place as somewhere I'd been just days before with Olivia: the cove. The seafront. The café. Perhaps I always would. Good. I had to remember Olivia every chance I could. I must not forget her, ever again.

Before I knew what was happening, the doorbell of Teddy's tinkled and Mum was walking inside.

'Mum, wait …'

Mum rubbed my arm. She knew I did not want to go in. I had spent so much time in here, with Olivia. I couldn't see that stupid mural, or the aluminium tables and chairs without my best friend.

'I'll treat you.' Mum smiled. 'Anything you want.'

Sighing, I trudged in after her. At the counter was a new girl. Her hair was dyed purple her face chock-full of piercings, a large tattoo on her right arm. She gave us a bright smile as she cleaned the counter.

'What happened to Ray?' I enquired, unable to help myself.

'He was turning the milk sour.' The girl indicated the menu, all the cakes on the counter in the glass case. 'What can I get you?'

The café was unusually busy, most of the tables occupied.

'What are you having, Jaz?' Mum said.

I thought of Olivia and what she would have chosen. 'Hot chocolate and sprinkles, with a cinnamon swirl, please.'

Behind us, the door opened again and the bell above tinkled …

Truth or Dare

'Truth is, everyone is going to hurt you.
You just have to find the ones worth suffering for.'
– *Bob Marley*

Twenty-Five

Saturday, August 25th

… As the bell sounded, time seemed to slow down. I tried to take a breath, yet air didn't fill my lungs. Panic blossomed in my chest, but was gone just as quickly. Colours exploded in front of my eyes, then Teddy's turned white.

'Hey, those for me?' Someone says, pointing a stubby finger at the hot chocolate and cinnamon swirl.

My vision returned with shocking clarity. I could see Olivia standing to the side of me. I was overjoyed to see her. I flung my arms around my best friend.

'What's all this for?' Olivia laughed.

As I let go of her, I realised I didn't know why I was so pleased to see Olivia, either. I was acting weird. I had only seen her the day before. *Hadn't I?*

I looked to the space to the other side of me. I had been sure Mum was there a moment ago. But no, there she was: I could see her across the road, moving displays out the front of Flossie's. Mum saw me and gave me an enthusiastic wave, completely uncool. I pretended to miss it.

'I've been calling you.' Olivia was wearing a leather

jacket over her long tee shirt dress. It gaped at the bust, showing the crossover of her bra.

'I must have left it on silent.' I patted my jeans back pocket, pulling my phone from it. Yep, there were missed calls and texts on screen.

'What a dump.' Olivia cast an eye around Teddy's. 'You know what this town needs? Somewhere cool for teens to go. Leather sofas, pool table, that kinda thing. They'd make a mint.'

I nodded, distracted. Olivia's idea sounded good, but there was something I needed to tell her … I couldn't put my finger on what.

'What are you doing here, anyway?' I said.

'You texted me?' Olivia grinned. 'About half an hour ago. Told me to meet you here. Honestly, you are being really strange.'

I still felt odd, but I had no reason to think Olivia was lying. I'd handed over the hot chocolate and cinnamon swirl, I never ordered stuff like that. Chatting about nothing like best friends do, we sat down at one of the aluminium chairs and tables.

'So, what's the plan?'

'… The plan?' Guilt lanced me in the stomach, though I was not sure why.

'Andrew Franklin said there's a party tonight,' Olivia's voice was wary: '… At Ellie's?'

Oh. That. *Of course.*

Ellie's demand came crashing back to me: *You tell her or I will.* Well, screw that. Olivia was my best friend. There was no way I was doing Ellie's dirty work for her! Better just to opt out altogether.

'Oh, really?' The lie by omission felt heavy on my

tongue. 'Dunno if I can bothered going out tonight.'

Olivia's mouth gaped open in disbelief. 'Are you serious!'

I picked at my jacket hem, unsure why the party had failed to raise my interest. Yet for some reason I just couldn't summon up the enthusiasm. Perhaps it was knowing Ellie would be on full show-off mode: *Look at me!*

'Fine, then I won't go.' Olivia sat back in her chair.

I shrugged, not bothered.

Olivia pursed her lips, aware her double-bluff had not landed home. 'Jaz! C'mon, don't be such a square. You know Ellie doesn't like me. I can only go if you do.'

I raised both palms in surrender. 'Why are you so bothered, anyway? You don't like Ellie, either.'

'Of course I don't, she's a two-faced ho who loves herself. But that family is minted. There's bound to be loads of booze and stuff. And apparently the parents won't be chaperoning. This is going to be the biggest party Winby will see all year!'

Just then, the bell above the door tinkled again. Niall wandered in, hands in pockets, that lopsided smile on his face.

'Hello, ladies.'

He made a beeline for our table, planting a kiss on my lips. He didn't sit down. Olivia looked on with a delighted smile. I may have never been able to figure out where I was with Niall, but even I couldn't deny he was hot as hell.

'You been avoiding me?' He leant on the table, gave me a pointed glance, 'You know, since …?'

'No, of course not.' I cut in, anxious to cut that avenue down.

'Good.' Niall sniffed. He remembered Olivia was sitting

opposite me and tipped her imaginary hat. 'I have to go, but you're both coming tonight, right?'

''Course. See you then.' Olivia flashed him her pearly whites, then pounced as soon as he meandered towards the counter. "Since'--what'? What was he talking about? Have you slept with him? Because if you have and you haven't told me, I will legit punch you in the face.'

'No!' The truth burst out of me, but my cheeks burned red with it. 'Honest!'

Olivia's brow creased, she didn't believe me. 'You better not be lying.'

She rose from her place. I watched her. She stood, hands on hips, eyes boring into me, as if I were breaking best friend protocol. Finally, she decided I was telling the truth.

She rolled her eyes at me. 'C'mon then, we need to get ready!'

I looked at my watch. It was only half two. 'We have ages yet.'

'Oh Jaz. You have so much to learn!' Olivia shook her head.

Cackling with laughter, she skipped out of Teddy's, forcing me to follow.

Twenty-Six

'Let's go back to yours.'

I wanted to get it over and done with as quickly as possible. I didn't want to hurt Olivia's feelings, but what was the point in playing the martyr? She couldn't go to the party. I couldn't change that. Olivia probably wouldn't even want to go anyway, she couldn't stand Ellie. But I *needed* to go! I had to make sure Becky and any of the other piranhas in Winby didn't crack on to Niall. Olivia would understand that in the long run.

'Hang on a sec, I'm hungry.' Olivia jangled a pocket full of change, heading towards The Penguin Fish Bar.

'Didn't you just have some chips?' A feeling of déjà vu hit me in the solar plexas. I felt as if we were retracing our steps somehow.

Olivia laughed at me. 'No? You're being so weird today, Jaz.'

I traipsed after her. The Penguin had been redecorated, a large banner reading 'UNDER NEW MANAGEMENT'. The Chos had moved out before the season had starte. They'd gone back to Glasgow and their extended family at the very top of the country. The new owners were a couple from Exmorton: he was tall and athletic-looking, his biceps covered in tattoos. She was short and always dressed in pink, with dyed blonde hair and huge talon-like nails that could barely hold the chip scoop.

As we wandered in, I noticed the new owners completely overhauled The Penguin. There was a proper seating area now, with large mirrored panels that made the shop look bigger. The Chinese lanterns were gone, replaced with cartoon goldfish and bubbles. Who'd want to eat a goldfish?

Olivia perused the menu. 'Can't believe they've discontinued the battered sausages, I reckon we should get compensation or something.'

The uber-pink woman appeared from out the back, an over bright smile on her fuschia lips that froze as soon as she heard Olivia's discontent.

'We're taking all feedback on board.' The pink woman said, adding extra chips to Olivia's portion, rolling it up in paper … Then unrolling it again as Olivia indicated she wanted them left open.

'Nothing ever stays the same, does it?' Olivia offered me a chip as we wandered back outside, towards the sea wall.

I picked one up and inspected it: white, underdone. Not remotely like the chips were before. I let it drop back on to the paper, uneaten. Olivia chattered away, but I barely listened.

How could I tell Olivia about her lack of invite to Ellie's party? Since my attempt to opt out and distract Olivia in Teddy's hadn't worked, I needed to find a way of getting through to her. I rehearsed it over and over in my mind.

The thing is Olivia … there's a party tonight and Ellie doesn't want you there.

No, too harsh. How about:

There's a party, but Ellie says she can only have a few

people round.

No, too soft! Olivia might not get the message that she absolutely couldn't go. I might be a coward, but I couldn't let my best friend walk accidentally into the lion's den. I could just imagine the look on Ellie's face! She'd want crush and humiliate Olivia if she did come, too. Plus Ellie would probably never speak to me again either. It was better for both of us if I just told her what Ellie said.

'Hey!'

Up the road, a figure disembarked from the Exmorton bus, a multitude of shopping bags in tow. She was wearing her hair in bunches, tied up with children's smiley face toggles.

Jenny Keller again.

She bounded up the street like that exuberant golden retriever we'd watched chase the ball on the beach that Christmas Day, years before. She stopped beside us on the seafront, nicking a lukewarm chip from under Olivia's nose. Like we were friends, or something. What the hell was up with this girl!

'Going to the party tonight?' There was a grin on Jenny's face as wide as the toggles in her hair. 'At The Grange. That grockle girl. Edie?'

'Ellie.' Olivia corrected Jenny. 'Yeah, probably.'

My best friend's brow furrowed at me. It was clear she was wondering if I had known about the party all along. Was I that transparent? Irritation itched between my shoulder blades, but then shame replaced it. Olivia had every right to doubt me. I *had* just spent the last twenty minutes trying to think of the 'right' way to break it to Olivia she couldn't go, for God's sake! But that wasn't my fault. I was piggy in the middle here.

'It's on Insta. And Snapchat. Even Facebook.' Jenny pulled a Native American outfit out of one of her shopping bags, complete with bow and arrow from her bag. *Seriously?* 'How wicked is this. Andrew's going as a Cowboy. Natch.'

Natch, I wanted to echo. But the news it was fancy dress did offer me a handy get-out clause. I pounced on it as Jenny gave us a cheery wave and set off for home.

'Oh no, that's us done then. I don't have anything. Too late to go into town now.' I painted on a disappointed face.

'Oh, we can knock something together.'

Foiled again!

Olivia looked across the road at the charity shop. The only one in Winby, it was the kind of charity shop that smelled of mothballs and cat pee, rather than the cool ones that competed with discount fashion stores for price-savvy bargain hunters.

I wrinkled my nose. 'Oh c'mon, that place is full of junk.'

It was true. Through the smeared glass of the shop window, a dummy wore long past-it wedding dress with pearl buttons to the neck and voluminous sleeves. It must have last been in fashion around the time my Mum was born, never mind us. At its feet were mismatched baskets of belts, shoes and Bric-A-Brac.

'Exactly!' Olivia grinned.

We opened the scarred, old door. Behind the counter, a middle-aged woman looked up from the paper. She wore too much bronzer, white lipstick and orange nails. Defiant, Olivia met her eye and stalked straight over to the wedding dress.

'What you reckon?' Olivia fingered the material.

The dress was stiff with age. It was meant for someone

about my size. It had been in the window so long, it was less ivory and more yellow.

'Me, a bride?' I raised an eyebrow. 'Who's the groom?'

'Me!' Olivia laughed.

She lowered her voice before the old dear behind the counter could say we were making too much noise and throw us out.

'I'll wear one of my Dad's suits. Zombie bride and groom. We'll be the best-looking couple there! C'mon. It'll be a laugh?'

It was a good idea… If we were both invited. But we weren't. Better to go with my original plan: persuade Olivia to forget about it, swerve the party.

'It's someone's wedding dress, doesn't seem right?' I stalled.

'They're probably divorced now. If I was divorced, I'd *want* my old dress to become a Zombie Bride! Wouldn't you?'

'*If* she's divorced.'

'She gave it to charity! She doesn't want it any more. Whoever she is, doesn't care!' Olivia called over to the old woman at the till who was staring at us. 'How much for the wedding dress?'

'Twenty.' The old woman licked her fingers and turned the page of her paper.

'I'll give you ten.'

The old woman blinked in surprise. Now Olivia had her attention. She pursed her thin lips, considering her next move.

'Fifteen.'

'Twelve.'

Olivia showed her the ten pound note from her pocket.

She nodded to me. I sighed and scraped through my purse. I manage to gather up two pounds in silver and coppers. I held it up: got it.

'Twelve pounds fifty and you've got yourself a deal, young lady.'

Olivia took her money and mine, plus another fifty pence and laid it all out on the glass counter in front of her.

'Let's get it down for you.' The old woman cracked a smile at last.

Five minutes later and the wedding dress was in our possession. ('We'll look after it,' I'd offered as we left. The old woman laughed and shook her head. 'Don't think I don't know what you're using it for ... You youngsters think we were born yesterday!'). Olivia had also found an old man's shirt and an incongruously jazzy tie on one of the hangers ('We can rip these!'), plus a battered bowler hat, which the old woman threw in for another two pounds.

'What about make up?' Olivia fretted.

It was too early for Halloween. As we stood on the seafront puzzling it out, Mum appeared on the steps of Flossie's with a box full of swim suits and flip flops.

'All right, girls!'

Mum was unusually cheerful as she replenished the display outside. Almost immediately two grockle parents swooped on some tiny swim shorts for their baby, cooing over how tiny they were. Their child – boy or girl, who could tell? - dozed in blissful ignorance in its pushchair.

'Hey Linda. Have you got any Halloween stuff in the stockroom?' Olivia enquired, forthright as usual.

Mum smiled. She was fond of Olivia. Sometimes I wondered if she'd prefer it if I were more like my best friend.

'No, sold it all off a while back. Why?'

'Party.'

Mum's expression twisted in confusion. 'Right. A Halloween party in August?'

'No, fancy dress. We're going as a Zombie bride and groom.' Olivia announced.

'Is that right …?' Mum looked to me, her expression difficult to read.

Was she annoyed I hadn't asked for permission? For a microsecond, my doomed heart leapt. Mum could ban me from going! Then I could avoid having to tell Olivia about her lack of invite AND save face with both Ellie and Niall: *Sorry, I'm grounded.* Of course, that left Niall wide open to the likes of Becky Jarvis, but I would just have to hope for the best.

'Oh. Sorry Mum. I won't go then.'

'… She can go, can't she Linda?' Olivia shrieked with indignance.

'Of course. Just wouldn't mind being reminded who runs the show round here, that's all.' Mum said, dry as ever.

My heart sank all over again. *How was I going to break it to Olivia now?* 'Hang on a sec, girls.'

Mum disappeared back inside the shop. We saw a light turn on upstairs, in the stock room. A few moments later Mum appeared with a box and handed them to us, with a smile. Inside: kids' face paints and brushes. Perfect for Zombie faces.

'Been upstairs for ages, never sold. You have them if you like.'

'Thanks, Linda!' Olivia threw her arms round Mum.

Mum laughed and returned the hug. 'Don't mention it.'

I stood on the sidelines, smiling too.

Now what?

Twenty-Seven

All the way back to hers, Olivia regaled me with her plans of how perfect we'd look. She said she'd backcomb my hair and add talcum powder for that 'aged' look. Also, what if I put some cornflakes on my face? Apparently, all the make-up artists in the movies used them for scabs and broken skin. It was a trade secret, she'd seen it on a DVD extra of some horror film.

I listened, glum at heart. Olivia was so excited. It didn't seem fair to have to break it to her she wasn't invited. But what could I do? If I didn't tell her, she'd be humiliated when Ellie wouldn't let her in. Talk about lose-lose.

'Olivia ...'

Olivia looked up from her Dad's old suit. It was one I'd seen him wear at a Christmas party years earlier, when Polly and Natalie were still at home. The house had been decorated with a theme. 'Winter Wonderland' Polly had called it, to anyone who asked. There were silver ribbons on the backs of chairs; Christmas wreaths on every available surface; matching tablecloth and napkins; small sparkling confetti in the shape of snowflakes. Polly had even called in a caterer.

She'd invited half of Winby, including Mum. She'd stood in the corner for most of it, apologising for Kevin who was uncharacteristically held up in Exmorton. Various text messages from him arrived giving her a countdown until he got there. But by the time Kevin arrived, the party had gone into full meltdown. Polly and Jim had got into a monumental row over the coats. An uneasy titter had worked through the small crowd as we'd listened to our hosts scream at each other upstairs. Ten minutes after that, people started to drift away, before even the canapés had finished serving. Kevin arrived just as me and Mum were gathering our things to leave, the last to go. I remembered looking back at Olivia and Natalie, my best friend with one arm slung around her little sister. Behind them a young, harassed waiter shovelled finger foods back onto platters to store in the refrigerator rather than waste. It had all been paid for, after all.

I inhaled a deep breath. 'I've got something to tell you.'

Olivia gave me an expectant smile.

Could I really do this to her? I would have to. I was looking out for her. It would be worse coming from Ellie, at the party, in front of everyone. That's what I had to remember. My mouth felt dry.

I hesitated. 'The thing is …'

'… Spit it out Jaz!' Olivia laughed.

My phone rang. Surprised, I fished it out of my pocket. On the screen, Ellie's name flashed. What the hell?

'Hang on …' Grateful for the distraction, I answered the phone. '… Hello?'

'Jasmine, hi.'

Ellie's voice sounded strange, as if she was trying to choke down laughter. In the background I could hear a low voice, though I couldn't make out any words. Was that Niall? Or Ste? Or someone else? There was a pause as Ellie cleared her throat.

'Look, Jaz. I've been thinking… about this morning. Well, I've changed my mind.'

'You have?' I was unsure what this turn of events meant.

'Well, Olivia can come. To the party I mean. Okay?'

My mind reeled. Ellie had been so certain this morning Olivia was not invited. What had changed? But I couldn't ask right now.

'I see,' I chose my words carefully, not wanting Olivia to guess what exactly we were talking about.

'So, make sure you bring her. Yeah?'

Ellie rang off. I stared at my phone a moment. What the hell had just happened?

'Who was that?'

'Oh, just Ellie. Checking we're coming.'

It was kind of the truth.

Olivia applied my makeup and did my hair, unaware of Ellie's change of heart. Next I did Olivia's hair and make-up, helping her on with her Dad's suit. She had to lie on the bed to do the trousers up, laughing the whole time. I dusted her lightly in talcum powder.

We'd spent all our money on the costumes, so we grabbed a bottle of vodka and one of sherry from Jim's not-so-secret stash in his bedroom, at the bottom of the built-in wardrobe.

'Won't he miss them?' I fretted.

Olivia shrugged, not caring. 'We're doing him a favour, drinking it for him!' She had a point.

Regarding ourselves in Polly's old full-length mirror in Jim's bedroom, we grinned at our reflections. We looked brilliant. I was relieved and grateful I hadn't told Olivia right away. For once, my hatred of confrontation had paid off!

Now, time for some fun.

Twenty-Eight

Music from The Grange echoed up Winby's long high street. Teens wandered right down the middle of the road, in costume. There were various hippies in bad wigs, flares and small round glasses. A lot of the lads were wearing togas, or their grans' dresses. Various curtains twitched as adults watched us, waiting for things to really kick off so they could spoil our fun. But that was hours away yet.

'What the hell are you?'

Olivia and I had fallen into step with Jake Harrington. He held a six pack of beer and was dressed in a white bin bag over his jeans and tee shirt.

'I'm a packet of crisps of course!' Jake grinned.

'Of *course*.' Olivia rolled her eyes.

Jake winked at us. 'So where are your costumes, girls … that's your normal Saturday get-up, right?'

'Oh very funny, hardy-ha!'

Olivia stuck her tongue at him, but she was still smiling. Jake was just ribbing us. He drifted away into the small crowd swarming up the steps to The Grange and through its open patio windows.

Olivia stopped to greet various people, engaging in momentary conversations before moving on. I followed her, sheep-like, unsure what else to do. I knew a lot of the people by sight, but not to talk to. Ste was up on the balcony, feet propped on the railings, pretending to read. I could see Jenny Keller standing on the patio next to the unlit barbeque pit with Andrew Franklin, her face already red and expression merry from drink. Sure enough, Jenny was dressed as a Native American, though Andrew's only concession to fancy dress was the cowboy hat on the top of his head.

I glanced around the rest of the patio. There was a handful of Sports Ed boys. All of them were in their best shirts, far too cool for fancy dress. I wondered briefly where Nat Williams was. It was not like him to miss a party. There were a couple of girls from my Biology class dressed as fairies; I only remembered their names because they were both called Kate. There was also a lad from my tutor group: Michael? Martin? I wasn't sure. He leant against the wall next to the patio doors, chugging back on a bottle of beer. He worse a stripy jumper and an eye patch, a plastic sword in his belt: a pirate, obviously.

Niall was nowhere to be seen.

Nor was Becky Jarvis.

'Jasmine! Livvy!'

From nowhere, Ellie swooped on us both. She was wearing a long red dress and cape. Red Riding Hood. She looked fantastic, of course. In an instant, I felt completely ridiculous.

'SO glad you could both come!' Ellie grabbed me and planted two kisses on my cheeks before I could move away. She attempted the same on Olivia who managed to dodge her just in time. Ellie's lie about wanting Olivia there felt as indelible as the red lipstick smear on my cheek.

'Wow. Great costumes.'

Another girl moved out of the shadows. She was dressed as a mermaid. She had an impossibly small bikini on her tiny frame, shimmering tail resting on her feet. She was smoking a cigarette and holding a pint glass in her small hand, her little finger poised as if it were a champagne flute. From her tone and impassive expression, it was impossible to tell whether she was complimenting us for real.

Olivia assumed she was not. 'We think so.'

My best friend looked to me for back up. But I said nothing, as ever.

Ellie tittered. 'Guys, meet my friend Vic. She's my bestie, back in London.' She looked back to Vic. 'Olivia's the one I was telling you about?'

A sudden pang of danger lanced my heart. What was that supposed to mean? Something about the look Ellie and Vic exchanged felt suss, especially after the sudden about-face on the phone earlier. For a moment I felt sure Ellie was setting Olivia up, but I wasn't sure how.

'There you are!'

Hands grabbed my shoulders: Niall. At last. He was dressed in green and had green face paint on. Was he a soldier in camouflage? Behind us, Ellie and Vic moved away, heads together. Olivia tapped me on the shoulder and gestured she was going to get a drink.

'Kermit,' Niall said, like he could read my mind. ' … The frog?'

I smiled. 'Worst. Costume. Ever.'

'Yeah okay, it's crap. All I could think of with what was in my wardrobe!' Niall laughed, though with the music so loud I couldn't hear it.

I squinted at him, lip-reading in the dimmed lighting. I could imagine myself, kissing those perfect lips. He could imagine it too, within seconds our faces were close together.

'You look fantastic. But then, you always do.'

Niall moved closer to kiss me. I wanted to, but I turned my face away at the last possible moment, embarrassed. He pulled his face away, his expression annoyed. He said something that was snatched away aby the music, though I saw the words formed by those lips:

Why are you always like this??

Like what??

I knew deep down what Niall meant though. The words stung, but truth always did. I was suspicious of him, even though he'd been nothing but nice to me. It wasn't him, it was me. I just couldn't believe someone like Niall would want to be with someone like me. I figured he had to have an ulterior motive, that he would let me down the first chance he got. But this was me, all over. I was standoffish with Niall, just as I was with everyone at college. I made out like I didn't need anyone, because that way people never got close enough to hurt me. I looked at Niall's imploring eyes and wanted to say all of this to him. But I couldn't.

So, I just shrugged.

'Oh, what's the point.' Niall's expression twisted from annoyed to hurt. He turned and pushed his way through the crowd on the patio, away from me.

What had I done??

I attempted to make my way after him, but people kept getting in the way. I was swept backwards, towards the house. A break in the music allowed me to hear someone call after him and then I heard Ellie's voice beyond:

'Oh, just let him go. Moody arsehole.'

But that wasn't him. Ellie was projecting: she was the only 'moody arsehole' in the Mackintosh family.

I ducked into the house, climbing over drunk teens sitting on the steps. I made it the stairs and made my way to the landing where there was a window that overlooked the cove. I could see Niall down on the cove, walking out towards the tide that was retreating up around the headland. He was little more than a shadow, the bright lanterns on the not enough to illuminate him.

I had lost him.

'You're not allowed up here.'

I jumped. Niall and Ellie's older brother Ste was standing next to me at the landing window, a book in hand, guarding the upstairs balcony. He looked older than his twenty-one years. Standing so close to the party, drunken teens splay-legged on the stairs just inches away, Ste nevertheless seemed completely distant and detached. Just like me. Was I destined to end up just like him, alone, with only books for company?

'Sorry.' I averted my eyes, trying to move past him.

But Ste did not move. 'You should go after him.'

'I can't.' The words were automatic on my lips.

'Or won't?'

I opened my mouth to reply but stopped. Ste was right. I would not go after Niall. That was my choice. It might be a bad choice, but it was mine to make. Knowing what my problem was didn't make it any easier to combat. I knew my limitations. I couldn't make myself vulnerable by going after Niall, not when he could reject me. I'd had my chance and missed it. That was all there was to it.

Ste sighed and moved out of my way.

I picked my way back downstairs over arms and legs and ill-placed teens, pushing my way back through the masses to the patio. I looked at the clock as I went: a little after ten. We'd been at the party under two hours, yet it felt like forever.

I glanced around the living room, through to the kitchen, out ahead to the patio. I couldn't see Olivia anywhere. The familiar feeling of unease prickled through me as I remembered Ellie and Vic's weird behaviour earlier.

I made it out into the cool night air. The music was not quite as loud out on the patio. Teens were huddled around the lanterns and heaters, some smoking. Ellie stood next to the sea wall, her red hood up, the moon behind her. She cut an impressive figure, like something from a movie. For a moment I wished I were just like her. If I were as beautiful, I could be as confident as her! What must it be like to do and say whatever you want? Freedom, surely.

'Let's go.' A hand grabbed for me out of the darkness.

I turned to find Olivia next to me. Her face wild, eyes glassy. Tear marks tracked their way down her face, making clean spots in her Zombie make-up.

I caught hold of her, by her shoulders. 'What's the matter? What's happened?'

Olivia shook her head. She didn't want to talk about it, not here. That feeling of trepidation I had earlier seized me, followed swiftly by anger.

'You're not going, I hope?' Ellie materialised next to us, arms folded.

Olivia swallowed. 'Fuck off, Ellie.'

'But it was just getting fun.' Ellie flashed those brilliant white teeth.

I looked to both of them, confused.

'What's Ellie said?' I demanded, before a realisation settled in my brain. This went way beyond words, it had to. 'Olivia, what has she *done*?'

Twenty-Nine

'Have a drink with me.' Ellie smiled, as if butter wouldn't melt.

She extended an arm towards us, glass in hand. Before of us could take it or object, Vic appeared in a flash of sequins, snatching it from Ellie.

'Don't mind if I do!' Vic's cool tone was more high-pitched. She was drunk.

Olivia turned on her heel to leave, still holding my hand. But before she could drag me away, a tall, broad guy in a wolf mask and black jumper appeared out of the darkness. He pulled off his mask and gave us all a dazzling white smile. Underneath, he was gorgeous: blonde hair, perfect teeth, impeccable skin. Male model material.

Nat Williams.

Olivia's face fell at the sight of him. She looked both panicked and frightened. In contrast, both Vic and Ellie seemed enthralled by his arrival. I knew something was about to happen, but I was the only one who didn't know what it was.

Nat cocked his head at her. 'Olivia.'

'Screw you, Nat.' She pointed at him, then at Ellie and Vic. 'And as for you two …!'

'What is it!' I was unable to keep the intrigue in any longer.

'It's done.' Nat said to Ellie.

'No way.' Vic breathed, '… I want proof?'.

Nat reached inside his pocket and pulled from it a girl's bra. I recognised it in an instant. I'd seen it that afternoon, as we'd pulled her into her Dad's suit. It had been white lace once, but after a red sock had made it into the whites wash courtesy of Jim, it was now pink.

Olivia's bra. *What the hell?*

Vic snapped her fingers. 'Give the man his money.'

'Fair is fair.' Nat's smirk split his face in two.

Even then, I was too naïve to understand they meant. Wide-eyed, I watched as Ellie grabbed her purse. She presented Nat with a ten-pound note.

Sickened, I realised with a thud what the trio had done: they'd made a bet on whether Nat could get Olivia into bed. Again. Just like he had at the party last year, when he was going out with Jenny Keller. How could she go there again??

I rounded on my best friend. 'You slept with him? *Here?'*

Olivia's eyes bulged. 'You're not even going to ask me what *really* happened? He held me down and took it!'

'As if,' Vic sniffed. 'Sluts gotta party. Just admit it, you got jiggy.'

'No, because it's not true!' Olivia shrieked.

'Well I was there. A bet is a bet!' Nat grabbed the note, held it under his nose like he was smelling it. 'It was fun, Olivia.'

Olivia was lost for words, for once. Vic's stare on her back, Ellie just shrugged. A cruel sneer was etched on her red lips. The music had stopped and no one had started it up again. Partygoers ventured to the patio doors to see the impasse between me, Olivia, Ellie and Nat.

'How could you?' Olivia repeated.

Jenny Keller seemed to flinch at my best friend's words. Olivia jerked away from her. My best friend ran into me, shouldering her way past me on purpose, before making her way down the patio steps and towards the high street. I stared after Olivia, watching helpless as she disappeared into the night, her words echoing around my head. *How could you?* Too late, I realised she had not been asking Vic, Ellie or Nat.

It was me.

Thirty

'Well that couldn't have gone better.'

Vic moved in front of Nat, who had already been distract-ed by some of his boys. I saw them all crowd in around him, clapping his arms and back. My mind reeled. Did they know what he had just done? Was this why Nat had done it? Or was he as much of a puppet as Olivia, thanks to the two bitches in front of me?

I grabbed Ellie by the arm. 'Why would you do that?'

Ellie looked uncertain for a micro-second. She'd seemed stricken when Olivia had run from the patio, but her usu-al impassive nonchalance had returned quickly. Now, she looked to Victoria, then back at me, defiant.

'… Because it's funny?'

I felt something snap, deep inside me. A shriek sounded across the patio and cut through the night. I barely realised it came from me.

I launched myself at Ellie, who was nearest to me, though in truth my rage was directed just as much at Vic. All the frustrations and hurt of the summer on Olivia's be-half hit me at once. Red mist clouded my common sense. I flailed wildly, raining blows on Ellie.

'You … bitch!' I screamed.

Caught unawares, Ellie staggered backwards towards the sea wall. Too late, someone shouted a warning and I realised what I was doing … But not before Ellie teetered backwards.

For a moment everything seemed to freeze.

I ran forwards. I grabbed at the air, missing Ellie's hand. She fell backwards off the sea wall, down into the cove. Her scream cut off abruptly as she hit the rocks below. An appalled hush reigned for a few microseconds.

What had I done??

'Oh my God.' Jenny Keller breathed, breaking the silence and prompting others to action.

'Someone call an ambulance!' Vic yelled.

I just stood there, helpless, not knowing what to do. One of the two Kates punched 999 into her phone. Accusing eyes glared at me. Various girls were berating me, but I could barely hear them above the sound of my own internal horror.

Teens scrambled down off the sea wall and down the rocks, towards Ellie's unconscious form below. Niall appeared too on the cove, his eyes locked with mine.

'What have you done?' He shouted ahead urgently as he ran towards his sister's prone body: 'Don't move her! Don't! We don't know if her neck's broken.'

I tried to say something, but no words came out. I stared down, over the sea wall, unable to defend my actions. They had no defence.

Neck. Broken. I could barely process it. It felt like a bad dream. I can't have almost killed Ellie … Could I? Shocked and disgusted with myself, I drifted away from the scene unnoticed, down the patio steps and back to the high street.

Thirty-One

I needed someone to tell me it was just an accident. That I hadn't meant it, that it could have happened to anyone. I went straight to Olivia's house. Standing outside her darkened bedroom, I willed her to come to the window.

'What do you want?'

Olivia made me jump. She appeared from the garden gate and the shadows, a cigarette in hand. She seated herself on one of the many large, empty flowerpots dotted outside the house. Once upon a time they'd all contained luscious arrangements and were tended to daily by Polly. But they'd died, neglected, when she'd left.

I wanted to tell her about Ellie. But I couldn't find the words.

'I wasn't in on it, you know. The bet, I mean.' I found myself saying instead.

Olivia took a last drag from her cigarette and ground the stub underfoot. She flicked her lighter, on and off, the wheel sparking in the gloom. Over our heads there was a full moon, watching us like a pale reproachful eye in the sky.

'Weren't you?'

'Of course not! I'd never do that to you.'

Olivia smiled, rueful. 'But you assumed I was at fault, right? Slutty Olivia, going off with Nat Williams. What did I expect?'

Guilt lanced my heart. Olivia was right. My first thought had been blame. Even when I'd been faced with hard evidence that she had been done over by Vic, Ellie and Nat! Some friend I was.

'I know. I'm sorry.'

'Except it doesn't mean much, does it?' The bitterness in Olivia's voice was unmistakable.

I did not like the sound of this. 'I can make it up to you?'

'No. You can't.' Olivia said slowly, as if she was explaining something to a small child. 'You see, sometimes there's only once chance. You get judged in that moment. There are no do-overs. I needed you and you let me down. That's all there is to it.'

I opened my mouth to argue with her, but I felt footsteps crunch behind me. They were accompanied by a burst of static. I turned and saw Jim behind us, his police uniform tucked hastily into his waistband, radio in hand.

'Jasmine. You need to come with me.'

My mind reeled for a moment: what could Jim want with me? Then with a sickening thud I realised. It was my fault Ellie had fallen. I had serious questions – legal questions – to answer.

Olivia bristled, surprised and irritated with her father. 'What's going on?'

'Go back inside.' Jim said, with typical indifference. He pressed a button on his radio. '… Yes, I've got her. Over.'

'Are you going to arrest me?'

I saw Olivia's eyes widen, her expression. She could not believe I could do anything so wrong. But then, as early as an hour ago, I hadn't either.

'That depends.' Jim said.

'Will someone tell me what is going on!' Olivia wailed.

I told Olivia I would explain everything in the morning. I felt strangely calm. Hadn't I been waiting for someone to come, make me answer for what I'd done? Maybe that was why I'd gone to Olivia's in the first place, so Jim could find me.

Jim showed me to his police car. He opened the door for me and I got in. Olivia stood in the driveway, watching, perplexed. Jim turned the key in the ignition and pulled out, taking the short trip down past the seafront to the station at the top of The Mount.

As we passed, I could see the cove was a hive of activity: an ambulance, its blue lights flashing round, its siren off, stood outside the pub. Drinkers crowded on the pub steps. They watched paramedics battle up the beach steps with El-lie, strapped into a gurney, a neck collar on. Niall and Ste hovered over their sister, faces ashen. Teens milled about, not sure what to do, yet still unable to tear themselves away. I looked at the clock on the dashboard. It was midnight.

A new day, yet already everything was ruined by a single moment of madness.

Mine.

Thirty-Two

I thought Jim would take me straight to the station. To my surprise, he took me home. He did not allow me to use my key, pressing the doorbell instead. Mum came to the door, sleepy-eyed and yawning.

'What's happened?' She demanded. 'Are you okay, Jaz?'

Of course Mum would think something bad had happened to me, not that I had caused it. Guilt lanced my heart. I attempted to tell her I was fine, but the lump in my throat was too painful. I just nodded. She looked me up and down. I was still in that ridiculous Zombie Bride outfit.

'Let's go inside, shall we.' Jim said. It wasn't a question.

Confused, Mum showed him in, babbling something about getting him a coffee, which he refused. The pair of us sat down on the sofa, Mum sitting next to me, her hand instinctively on my elbow.

Jim sat opposite in the threadbare armchair. 'There's been an incident ...'

'Well, obviously.' Mum interrupted, anxious he spit it out.

'... Hasn't there, Jasmine?' Jim's gaze fell on me, his meaning clear: *tell your mother.*

I drew a shaky breath. I wasn't sure I could put into

words what I had done. I could barely believe it myself. It felt preposterous, like a bad dream. I wasn't a violent person. Yet I had caused Ellie to fall. I couldn't bear the thought of horror and disappointment replacing the earnest expression on my mother's face.

'I'm sorry, Mum.' I burst into tears.

Half an hour later and Jim left, leaving an appointment card with us. We were to go to Winby police station in the morning. 'Voluntary attendance' he called it, which 'negated the need for an arrest', apparently.

Still in shock, Mum nodded. She said I would be there and I would answer all the police's questions. She closed the front door and leant against it, staring into space. Still on the sofa, I stared at Mum, silently willing her to say something.

'Mum …?'

I was afraid to break the silence, yet felt compelled to do it anyway. I needed her to say she knew I hadn't meant it; that she realised it was an accident; that everything would be okay.

But Mum did not look at me … *Could not look at me?*

'Go to your room, Jasmine.' She looked down at the appointment card in her hand, as if willing it to disappear.

'Mum.' I was shocked. I had imagined tears, recriminations, proclamations.

'Now.' She said, through clenched teeth.

I trudged to my room, shutting the door behind me. My own mother had rejected me! I couldn't believe it.

Catching sight of myself in the mirror, I realised I was still in fancy dress. I was struck by how ridiculous I looked. With a howl, I wrenched the zip of the bridal dress, yanking it off, not caring when I heard the fabric rip. I grabbed a hairbrush and pulled it through my tangled hair. Next I set to work on removing my makeup. Finished, I regarded myself in the mirror, fresh-faced in just my underwear. I looked haunted. *What had I done?*

I fell on the bed. I had a couple of hours of fitful sleep. I dreamt I was on board a shipwrecked ocean liner. It was a huge beast made of iron and steel, broken open like a plastic bath toy against the rocks. Olivia was there and so Ellie. None of us knew why the ship had run aground. There was no one aboard except us. We were somewhere below deck and the ship was flooding. Though we climbed ladder after ladder, attempting to reach safety, we just couldn't find the top deck.

Water kept pouring in.

~

I awoke with a start to find Mum standing over me.

'Get dressed.' She had a weird expression on her face, as if she didn't recognise me.

Mum and I walked in silence to Winby police station. It was a tiny place, just a reception and a single interview room. I remembered a 'tour' back in primary school. It had been explained that Winby station was not a 'designated custody centre'. People who had been arrested had to be taken to Exmorton, where they had the real cells. Jim was not there. I envied him, presumably at home right now, still in bed. How I wished I could go back to my own and pull the covers over my head, pretend this was not happening.

A young police officer with braided hair signed us in. We sat opposite her on two plastic chairs. A tinny radio was playing jaunty pop songs, which seemed a bizarre contrast to how I was feeling. We were on time, but no one came for us. Beside the reception desk, dog-eared crime prevention posters lined the walls. There was also a near-empty rack of leaflets. I read them, over and over for quarter of an hour. Above the door of the interview room was an old style white clock, stained yellow with the passage of time. I watched the minute hand travel round its face for fifteen more minutes before finally saying something.

'I didn't mean it.' I declared, 'It was an accident.'

'I know …' Mum looked at me at last. My heart lifted for a microsecond, before she followed it up with: '… Still did it though, didn't you?'

Crushed, I felt my cheeks burn with shame.

I did not have time for a response. Another police officer came out of the interview room. Despite her customary uniform and bare cheeks and lips, I noted she must be quite glamorous off-duty. Her hair was dyed blonde; her skin was sun lamp -tanned; her hands and wrists bore the white marks of multiple heavy jewellery.

'Sorry about the wait.' The glamorous police officer said cheerily. 'Would you like to come in?'

No, I thought.

But I stood up with Mum anyway, following the first officer into the pokey little room. There was a Formica table with an old-fashioned tape recorder on it. Scarred paintwork on the walls. A narrow window that looked out on to The Mount. A guy with owl-like glasses sat at the table, shuffling papers and drinking coffee from a thermos flask. He stood up as we entered, offering his hand to shake, introducing himself as my duty solicitor, Bobby. No surname apparently.

The police officer with braided hair wandered in after us. She sat down in the corner of the room, her arms crossed as if awaiting a play at the theatre. The glam police officer introduced herself as Sergeant Thornton and her colleague as PC Bensham. Thornton read out a long spiel about why I was there and identifying who was there, 'for the benefit of the tape', just like on television.

Next, I was asked to confirm who I was. Mum was too. I was asked if I understood what the interview was about. I was advised that I was not under arrest and could leave at any time, though I was cautioned that anything I did not mention and later relied on in court may harm my defence. Court? I felt as if I was watching myself from above, or on television. None of it felt real.

'I did it.' I blurted out, drawing an alarmed expression from Bobby. He gestured something to Mum, but she ignored him and nodded to me. *Go on.*

'So, run us through what happened?' Sergeant Thornton said. Her previous cheery demeanour was gone. Her eyes were steely, deadly professional.

'Can I just point out Jasmine has no priors?' Bobby interrupted.

'We're aware. And can I point out Jasmine is not under arrest? It's up to her what she tells us.' Sergeant Thornton replied with a humourless smile. She ate solicitors for breakfast, especially ones straight out of university, like Bobby.

Face like thunder, Bobby clicked his pen, writing something down. 'If I may have a moment with Jasmine?'

'Of course.' Thornton said, standing up. PC Bensham followed her superior out without a word or backward glance.

'It was an accident.' My mother said, for the umpteenth time. 'It's surely better if Jasmine tells the truth?'

'Perhaps.' Bobby said. He was wearing a crumpled shirt

with a stain on the collar, which did not exactly fill me with confidence. But we couldn't afford legal representation, so had to rely on the one we were assigned. In Winby, there was not much choice. 'But the CPS may argue …'

'… CPS?' My mother said, exasperated, the subtext obvious: *Speak English.*

'Crown Prosecution Service.' Bobby said. 'They're the ones who decide whether charges should be brought and what those charges will be.'

'What's likely?' Mum fretted.

Bobby sighed. 'The more serious charge they may go for is Grievous Bodily Harm.'

'That sounds serious.' Mum groaned.

'It is serious. They could argue that at seventeen, Jasmine should have known her actions could result in serious harm to the other girl … Since she should have been aware Ellie was standing on the patio next to the sea wall.'

Mum nodded, her face drawn. My eyes went from adult to adult, unable to contribute.

Bobby coughed, still shuffling papers. 'GBH has two categories: with intent, or without. Either way, that would be heard before a jury at Crown Court. That said, we would hope that charge, if brought, would get downgraded to the lesser charge of Actual Bodily Harm …'

'Actual Bodily Harm.' Mum looked at me like she was seeing me for the first time. It was as if I had transformed before her eyes from the child she'd once known to a monster, overnight. *How could this be?*

'However, since Jasmine has no prior convictions I would hope for leniency.' Bobby said quickly. 'Along with expression of remorse, naturally.'

'Well she's sorry.' Mum interrupted. 'Very sorry. Aren't

you, Jaz?'

'Yes. Very sorry.' I echoed, speaking aloud at last.

Bobby pursed his lips and wrote something down. He didn't seem to care whether I was sorry or not.

Moments later, the door opened and Sergeant Thornton and PC Bensham came back in. This time, PC Bensham asked me a few questions about the party and Ellie, under Sergeant Thornton's watchful eye. Bobby nodded to me, giving me permission to answer. I expected the police-woman to make various barbed comments or attacks on me like they do on TV, but the PC made various notes without judgement. The end of the session seemed to come abruptly. After about an hour, we were told we could go. Just like that.

'Will she be charged?' My mother stopped at the desk on our way out. Bobby had already gone. His phone had gone off three times during our meeting. It must be tough being the only free brief in town.

'We don't know yet.' PC Bensham replied. 'That depends on what other witnesses to the event say.'

Another awkward silence descended between Mum and I as we left the station. In contrast to the dark mood between us, it was a bright, sunny morning at the top of the hill. From the station I could see the cemetery across the road, to the large concrete swan in front of the huge flowerbeds reading 'Welcome To Winby'. From there I could see down into the cove: the beach was clear of people, no trace of what had happened the night before.

'Mum?'

Mum walked slightly ahead, her head tilted skywards, looking at the blue sky, rather than me. 'Don't. Just don't, Jaz. All right?'

Hurt, I trailed after her, back to the flat.

Thirty-Three

I went straight to my room before Mum told me to. I flung myself on my bed and looked at my phone. There were no voicemails, no texts or notifications on the screen. No one even wanted to have a go at me for what I'd done. I was completely alone. Even my own mother was disgusted with me.

I couldn't blame them. All of this could have been avoided, if I had just done what I was supposed to: stick up for my best friend. How hard would that have been? We would never have been at the party, then. I'd not listened to my gut instinct when I'd wondered if Ellie was up to something. All the evidence had been there: the sudden change of heart; the laughter on the phone call; Ellie's pointed 'Olivia's the one I told you about?' What Ellie, Victoria and Nat had done to Olivia was terrible, but I was doubly at fault: first for letting Olivia down, then for attacking Ellie.

I sent a text to Niall: *HOW'S ELLIE?*

Unable to wait for the response, I decided to distract myself: I grabbed a towel, marching through the kitchen to the bathroom. I stood under the shower, letting it run as hot as I could stand, watching my skin turn pink and then red. Steam filled the bathroom; I couldn't see my reflection in the mirror when I got out.

I wondered what Kevin would say if he knew what I had done? Life seemed so much simpler when I was a child, as he read to me from his favourites every week, bringing the words to life. I wiped the mirror clear, wishing that like Alice I could escape through the glass into another world beyond. I would never come back.

The red light was blinking on my phone as I came back into my room, a reply waiting for me: *WHAT DO YOU CARE? N.*

Fighting back tears, I bit my lip and pressed in a reply: *OF COURSE I DO. I'M SORRY.*

But no reply came, then or hours later. Another text beeped that evening. I grabbed my phone, hopeful.

It was from Olivia. It read, *IS IT TRUE?*

I hesitated, not wanting to confirm that I had hurt Ellie, but I had no choice. I pressed the buttons and sent a reply: *YES.*

No more came from my best friend. I felt absurdly betrayed. But I could not blame Olivia. Even faced with Ellie, Vic and Nat's horrible actions, I had blamed my best friend first.

I deserved all I got.

~

Days passed. Mum was still ashamed of me and no word came from The Grange or the police. I thought everything would be quick, like all those crime series I had watched on TV. The long arm of the law appeared to work in slow motion in real life. Every morning I'd wake, heart hammering, sure that day would be the day I'd hear whether I was going to be charged or not, wondering whether I'd go to prison.

I read online and in the paper about my case, though no names were mentioned as we were all still under eighteen. I got my only updates from the articles. Ellie had received a depressed skull fracture but was going to be okay. I breathed a little easier then. I took a card to The Grange and popped it through the letterbox. It was returned hours later, put back through the flat door. Soon after, the Mackintoshes packed up The Grange and left for London, a large 'FOR SALE' sign left behind in the window.

The new term started, but college told me not to come in. They told me I had not been expelled, but that I had to 'make my own arrangements for my education'. I had been cut adrift from my own life. I felt relief at not having to face everyone, but frustrated that I was stuck. I desperately wanted to escape, just like in my shipwreck dream, but I could not find my way out of the nightmare.

Finally, the phone call came.

It was a Friday. Mum carried her mobile everywhere with her, even to the toilet, for fear of missing the news we were waiting for. She snatched up the phone as we always did now, even though nine times out of ten it was someone cold-calling insurance or double glazing.

But this time Mum didn't sigh, shoulders sagging. She tensed up, drawing my attention. I nodded at her so she could give me some indication, but instead she just waved me away.

' … Okay. Thank you very much.' Mum was giving nothing away.

I waited. My heart sank, sure it was bad news. Mum hung up and looked at the phone, as if she couldn't understand it.

'Well?' I thought I already knew the answer. The police

would arrive, any second and arrest me.

'They're not bringing any charges.' Mum's relief seemed to flood out of her.

'What?' I had been so sure of the opposite, I could not believe what Mum had just said. 'How?'

'Not in the public interest, they said.' Mum's own disbelief was evident.

We had a last meeting with Bobby not long after. He explained that cases were only brought when certain they could be won. On examining the evidence, it had been decided that though my actions were foolhardy, it had been a genuine accident, especially due to witness statements insisting I had 'barely touched' Ellie.

'Who said that?' I demanded.

'Ellie herself, apparently.' Bobby said.

I couldn't understand it. I knew I had struck Ellie hard; I could remember doing so. I had been livid with her over the bet and furious with myself, for allowing it. Why would Ellie lie, when I *had* caused her accident? I should be punished for it!

Then I realised: I already had. The threat of a court case had hung over me for weeks; I'd lost all my friends, even Olivia. Even if I returned to college now, I'd be ostracised. It might be all over now, but the episode had damaged mine, Ellie's and Olivia's lives irreparably. We all had to live with that.

Back home, alone as usual, I grabbed my phone and tapped out a text message, sending it to Ellie: *THANK YOU*. No reply came, but I knew she would know why.

At home, step by step, I repaired my relationship with Mum. Though hurting Ellie had been the worst thing that had ever happened to me, it did make Mum see me differently at last. Mum had seen me as a little girl for so long, it was like I was frozen in time.

I started work at the chip shop with the lady in pink, Michelle. She wore a wig, to disguise the fact she'd lost her hair to chemo the summer before. Her hair was still short, but growing. She was in remission, she told me, but it had made her see everything differently. Michelle's tattooed husband was called Ricky, a giant of a man who'd once been a painter and decorator, but now turned his hand to fixing deep fat fryers. They had a daughter, Cassie, who was about my age and worked at the shop too. Over the weeks she thawed to me a little, though I wouldn't exactly say we were friends.

Outside work, I poured everything into my training, intent on making it to County Level and if I was lucky, beyond. As the months passed, I got faster and faster. I no longer felt as if I was outrunning my shame. I would sometimes see Olivia, usually getting on or off the college bus at the clock tower, sometimes in step with Jenny Keller. I would always wave. In time, they started to wave back.

One afternoon on the seafront, I slowed down as I ran past, falling into step with them both. Olivia gave me a wan smile, but Jenny as always flashed me her wide grin.

'How's it going?' Jenny said.

'All right.' I said. And meant it.

'What's your time?' Olivia said in a quiet voice.

'Let's get a drink and I'll tell you.' I gestured towards Teddy's as we found ourselves outside. At the back of the queue, Andrew and Jake waved to Jenny, beckoning her inside.

Olivia looked as if she was going to say 'Thanks, but no thanks'. But then the bell on the door tinkled as Jenny

pushed it inwards, leaving me and Olivia on the threshold.
'Okay, but you're buying.' Olivia said to me …

Spin The Bottle

'I shiver, thinking how easy it is to be totally wrong about
people—to see one tiny part of them
and confuse it for the whole, to see the cause and think
it's the effect or vice versa.'
- *Lauren Oliver*

Thirty-Four

Saturday, August 25th

… As the bell above the door rang over our heads, everything seemed to come to a standstill. I felt as if I was lurching backward, then pulled and fast-forwarded. It felt like I was a character on screen in one of those old VHS machines.

In the blink of an eye, I was no longer by the door of the café. Instead I was seated across the room, sitting down myself. On the table, two phones, two hot chocolates, one still full. Across the aluminium table from me: Olivia, pouring sugar from the shaker, creating patterns on the metal tabletop.

'… Don't you reckon?'

Olivia wasn't looking at me, so didn't notice my sudden confusion. Why wasn't she affected? What the hell had just happened? I took a deep breath, attempted to calm the fluttering sensation in my chest. I was overtired, being ridiculous. I must have imagined it.

'Sure.' I hoped that answered the question.

It seemed to. Olivia carried on chatting as I looked around the café. We were not the only ones there. A teen girl sat at one of the tables, a small toddler resting on her lap. Across the table, a lad sat awkwardly, trying to engage with the little boy, who hid his face in his young mother's neck. Behind the counter, Moody Ray mixed milkshakes for a Mum and a little boy of about eight. Another teen girl was seated alone at her table, sketching. She had sandy hair cut short, piercing green eyes and a chain running from the top of her ear to the bottom. I'd seen her hanging around the Penguin Fish Bar.

'So, what's the plan?' Olivia caught my attention again at last.

All the pieces fell into place. I remembered going running that morning across the cove, going up to see Ellie afterwards. Talking with her in the kitchen at the breakfast bar. Ellie telling me about the party, her plans for that night … And how Olivia was not invited. I glanced at my phone. Yup, in black and white and emojis, Ellie's threat: *YOU TELL HER OR I WILL.*

Sigh.

Resentment and realisation washed over me. This wasn't on. Ellie had been a total bitch, all summer. I had been a crap friend to Olivia.

Time to stand up for my best friend.

~

'This place is so dull!'

It was about ten days after Ellie and the rest of her family had moved into The Grange. She lay on her bed amongst a swathe of teenage magazines and other junk: emery boards, bottles of nail polish, hairbrushes.

'What do you guys do for fun round here?'

'Go down the cove?' I replied, flicking through one of the magazines.

'I meant grown up fun?' Ellie growled. 'Not drinking cider on the beach.'

I winced. 'There's Red and Blacks?'

Red and Black's was Winby's only nightclub. Given its lack of viable clientele, it was possible to get in and be served at the bar with a photocopied ID.

'Spare me.'

Ellie had seen the noticeboard outside Red and Black's advertising meat draws in-between posters for speed dating and eighties nights. Mum and her best mate Kelly (whose brother was Uncle Tim, who wasn't my uncle) went to the last speed date night and discovered they'd outnumbered the men four to one. They'd collapsed into the flat past midnight, waking me up to help them set up our ancient Wii to play Just Dance. Competitive as ever, four hours later I had completed all the dances, whilst they'd crashed out on the sofa and flicked peanuts at me to put me off. I'd thought that was a good night.

But Ellie was used to a different standard of nights out – or in. 'What about the nightclubs in Exmorton?'

I thought of the clubs on The Strand, down by the quay. The exclusive guest lists, the bouncers outside. 'We'd never get in.'

Ellie smirked. 'Yeah?' She whipped out some ID from her purse: it was fake – *Ellie, nineteen? Don't think so* – but absolutely perfect in every way. She'd even laminated it. Official.

'Where did you get that?' I breathed.

'Internet.' Ellie grinned. 'Let's get you one.'

Half an hour later and I had one too. I couldn't wait to

show Olivia. 'We can go to the clubs on The Strand?'

'They're full of freaks.' Olivia declared. 'Besides, taxis back here past midnight cost a bomb.'

'Ellie's paying.' I said.

Olivia weighed it up. 'You can only stay out until midnight … What would your Mum say?'

'I could tell her I'm staying at yours.' I wasn't allowed to stay at The Grange. My Mum had seen Ellie had two older brothers.

Olivia sucked her cheeks in. 'I don't like lying to Linda, she's all right.'

'I wouldn't be lying,' I said, 'I *would* be staying at yours … Just not all night?'

Olivia's wary expression became a wide grin. 'Now you're talking.'

Later on, Ellie opened the door to The Grange. Her smile froze on her face at the sight of my best friend.

If Olivia noticed, she made out she didn't. 'Hey Eleanor.'

It was some sort of one-upmanship to them: Ellie always shortened Olivia's name, so Olivia lengthened Ellie's. I groaned inwardly. Maybe this *was* a mistake.

'Hi.' Ellie said through gritted teeth. 'Jasmine, help me in the kitchen?'

I traipsed into the kitchen after Ellie. On the counter was a two six-packs of beer and a bottle of vodka, plus two cartons of orange juice.

'What's *she* doing here?' Ellie unscrewed the vodka cap and poured herself a large measure.

I tried to change the subject. 'Niall not in?'

'He's gone into town ahead of us.' Ellie chucked in some orange juice with the vodka, then chugged the lot. '… So?'

'You know I can't stay here,' I pointed out, 'I have to

stay at Olivia's.'

'So go there after, don't bring her along. God.' Ellie grimaced as the vodka went down neat this time. 'She doesn't even have ID I bet.'

'Olivia doesn't need ID.'

This much was true. With her ample bosom and seemingly never-ending well of confidence, Olivia could get in anywhere she wanted.

'Might come in handy?'

Ellie considered this for a moment. It did make sense.

'Fine.' She said, 'She can come.'

'Starting without me?' Olivia turned up, eyes wide, looking from me to Olivia. Ellie's flashed her a fake smile. 'Not at all.'

She pushed full glasses towards us both. Vodka and orange at the ready, Ellie proposed a toast: 'To the best night out ever.'

We clinked glasses.

~

I made my decision. I was overthinking all this. Ellie had backed down last time, when we'd all gone out in Exmorton, quick enough. Plus I'd screwed up that night with my best friend, the least I could do was stand up for her now. I would go to the party ... WITH Olivia.

'Ellie's having some sort of gathering. Wanna go?'

Olivia's brow furrowed. ' ... And she wants me there, after last time?'

So, Olivia hadn't entirely forgotten our jaunt to The Strand either. I couldn't blame her. I took the plunge.

'No.' I admitted. 'In fact, she told me you weren't invited and not to bring you under any circumstances.'

Olivia pursed her lips. 'Sounds about right. What do you think?'

'I think she can go fuck herself.' I kept a straight face.

Olivia cackled with glee. 'Holy crap Jaz, did you just swear AND mug Ellie off in one sentence?'

I shrugged, a smirk on my own lips.

Olivia slammed both palms down on the aluminium table. 'I think we should go.'

I thought Olivia might suggest this. 'It'll be crap.'

'You know it won't. You're just saying that, for me.' Olivia's words hit home, 'Besides, I know you want to go, Niall will want you there too.'

It was true. Niall's message had come in after Ellie's: *TONITE WILL BE FUN?* The question mark was a weird addition. Had he thought it might *not* be fun? Or maybe it was because of what happened between us last time, after The Strand.

'Come on.' My mind made up, I stood. 'Let's get ready at my place.'

'Is your Mum in?' Olivia grabbed her bag.

I shook my head. 'Double shift.'

Olivia dug something out of her bag. 'And look what I've got.'

A litre bottle of vodka. We high-fived.

'Let's go.' I said.

Thirty-Five

Back at mine, Olivia laid all my clothes on the bed to consider all the various combinations as we poured generous measures of alcohol for ourselves.

'What about this one?' Olivia held up a pretty dress with a floral pattern and halter neck.

'I'll just wear this.' I said, indicating my jeans and vest top.

'You will not.' Olivia huffed, ''C'mon, let's dress up a bit. This is going to be fun.'

I was unconvinced. The last time Olivia and I had gone out on a big night out had been a total nightmare. Ellie had been with us then as well. Now I thought of it, disaster seemed to follow that girl around like a dog.

What if tonight was the same?

~

Tipsy before we'd even left The Grange, all three of us had been high with excitement about going to Exmorton. As Ellie paid for the taxi with actual cash – '*I can't believe there isn't Uber down here!*' - Olivia helped me out of the vehicle so I didn't trip. I took in grateful gulps of the night air.

'You okay, Jaz?'

I was not okay. I had not eaten before going out. The vodka sloshed around in my stomach like gasoline. Groups of young people congregated outside various clubs, arguing their case with Bouncers: *Yes, they were eighteen. No, they weren't drunk.* Liars, all of them.

So was I. ''Course! I'm fine.'

'Is Niall meeting us at the club?' I hoped I sounded nonchalant.

'Dunno. He's meeting some mates from uni.' Ellie made 'uni mates' sound as if they were four thousand miles beneath her somehow.

'From London?' I enquired.

'I don't know, do I?' Ellie said testily, 'From around. They're staying at the camp site outside Exmorton.'

Like children traipsing after their mother, Olivia and I fell into step with her. Ellie stalked towards the biggest, most exclusive club, Elemental. Elemental was a tall building with chrome fittings and ideas above its station: it looked like it had been transplanted from Manchester to little Exmorton. The girl on the bright shiny ticket booth wore a PVC bustier over her augmented breasts. The bouncers were decked out in black tie and earpieces. Ellie flashed a doorman with a thick, tattooed neck her most brilliant, dentist-white smile.

'Hi,' She was so sure her beauty would captivate him.

Unlucky for Ellie, he'd seen it all already. The Doorman looked her up and down, unimpressed. 'ID?'

'Of course,' Ellie produced hers and nudged me.

I scrabbled about in my bag for mine, the contraband bottles of vodka clinked together. Ellie shot me a look.

'No alcohol allowed in.' The Tattooed Barman said.

'W-We don't have any on us,' Ellie was reduced in an instant: smaller, flustered, less powerful.

The Doorman raised one eyebrow. 'Move along.'

'But …' Ellie's face flushed. I half-expected her to stamp her foot in a childish tantrum.

'Move along … Now.' The Doorman repeated.

Red-faced, Ellie stalked away. Olivia and I raced after her, joining the rest of the young people milling about. We assessed our options.

'Well. That went well.' Sarcasm oozed off Olivia in waves. 'Thought you had no problem getting into clubs in London?'

'You do better.' Ellie challenged.

Olivia grinned. '… Watch.'

We walked towards the next club. Smaller than Elemental, Tricky's was a complete dive. An unshaven bloke manned the ticket booth; a single, well-built Doorman in trackie bottoms leant against it. The 'r', 'y' and apostrophe on its neon sign was missing, so it read 'Ticks'. Olivia made a beeline for the ticket booth.

The Doorman in trackie bottoms made a half-hearted attempt to get in her way. 'Hi girls. Good night so far?'

'So-so,' Olivia said turning on the charm offensive, 'Better now, though.'

'Oh is that right … How come?' The Doorman smirked.

'For seeing you of course.' Olivia ensured the Doorman had a clear view down her cleavage. Ellie's eyes went out on stalks. I giggled, used to Olivia's tricks.

'I think that's my line. Go on, then!' The Doorman laughed, waving us through.

Olivia grinned triumphantly at a pinched-face Ellie, then handed our money over to the guy in the ticket booth. I just stood there, causing Ellie to push me forward and hurry me along before the Doorman could clock us.

We were in.

~

'These, together. With your purple Docs. You'll look gorgeous!'

Olivia held up purple corduroy skirt and a white vest top, with a purple shrug and a purple flower for my hair.

'I'll look like The Purple Murple.' I complained.

The Purple Murple was a supply teacher we'd had when we were at Winby High. No matter the weather, The Purple Murple would arrive at school not only dressed head to toe in purple, but carrying a purple bag, filled with a purple folder of work, complete with a purple pencil case filled with purple pens and pencils. She was just begging for the unwanted attentions of schoolchildren: 'Purple Murple' was one of the *kinder* names we'd had for her.

Olivia tutted and flung the purple shrug and flower down, replacing it with a dark blue cardigan and a blue shell necklace. '… Better?'

'Better.' I smiled, feeling the vodka create a warm sensation in my stomach.

As Olivia chatted happily about the party, Niall's face seared through my brain. We'd gone out since the night in Exmorton, but only for coffee, or a quick walk on the beach. I hadn't brought up what had happened that night, but nor had he. The look on his face – had it been disapproval? I realised that humiliation *had* made me avoid him. Suddenly he seemed so much older, wiser, more experienced than me … And I didn't like it.

'You okay, Jaz?' Olivia clocked my pensive expression.

'Absolutely.' I countered, holding my glass in the air. 'To us! Best friends forever.'

We clinked glasses.

Thirty-Six

Tipsy again, we made our way down to the seafront. Dark clouds gathered overhead, threatening rain. Even so, The Grange had all its French windows open and music blared across the patio. Someone sat on a sun lounger up on the balcony. It wasn't Ste for a change, or even Niall or Ellie, but a bony girl in a red bikini that looked too big for her. I shivered, even though I was wearing considerably more clothes. Didn't the bony girl know you couldn't get a tan without any sun?

I looked at my watch: it was past half eight, nearly nine. Ellie had specified eight, knowing no one in their right mind would come at that exact time … But surely her guests would be there by now? We trudged up the steps at the back of The Grange and knocked on the door.

'It's a disaster!' Ellie wailed as she opened the door. 'There's like, twenty people here!'

Twenty was a pretty good turn-out as far as I was concerned, but someone like Ellie was used to far bigger gatherings. Ellie's nostrils flared as she took in Olivia, shooting me a *'What the Hell?'* look. I merely grinned back as if I hadn't understood.

'People are dropping out like flies. I've had about fifty

texts in the last ten minutes.' Melodrama was Ellie's thing.

'Oh, I'm sure we can come up with something to do.' Olivia's eyes darting about the kitchen. On the counter were several cases of beer, three bottles of wine and two more bottles of vodka.

Behind her, a couple of teens were making themselves at home in the big open plan living room. I spotted Nat Williams, plus a couple of his rugby mates. There was Niall, Becky Jarvis and of course, Jenny Keller and Andrew Franklin. I was jarred to see Jenny, but I wasn't sure why.

The rest I didn't know their names, though I knew their faces, barring the girl in the red bikini. Book in hand, Ste opened the door to the kitchen and turned around just as quickly, not even bothering to try and look as if he was avoiding us all.

'Ste!' Olivia trailed after him into the living room. 'What are you reading?'

Ste merely held up the book as means of reply as he retreated up the stairs beyond: *Lord Of The Rings*. That figured.

'It's like a nerd apocalypse out there.' The skinny girl in the too-big bikini arrived in the kitchen. A towel was wrapped around her tiny waist. The right side of the bikini was slipping down, showing her nipple. I averted my eyes.

'Tell me about it.' Ellie said, weary. 'Vic – Jasmine. Jasmine – Vic.'

Ellie grabbed a bottle of peach schnapps, some orange juice and half a bottle of sugar syrup from the cupboard.

'You're from London?' I was anxious to make small talk and fill the empty silence.

Vic gave me a paper-thin smile. 'So, *you're* Jasmine.'

I wasn't entirely sure if it was a good or bad thing. 'Ellie mention me?'

'A little. Mostly that Olivia … That was the whale that just went after Ste, right?' Vic's smirk matched Ellie's.

I felt a pang of anger course through me. Whale? Who did this walking coat-hanger think she was!

'Olivia's not a whale.'

But Vic was not listening. She pulled on a tee shirt of Ellie's from an overflowing basket of clean clothes next to the sink. It was much too big for her and Ellie was tiny. That's how eye-wateringly small Vic was.

Ellie rifled through cupboards. She managed to source a bottle of ginger ale and jar of maraschino cherries from the back of one cupboard as she chattered away to no one in particular, least of all me.

'The only way to get through tonight is to get totally blotted.' Ellie dumped all of it into a large mixing bowl, plus the schnapps and sugar syrup, mixing it with a large soup ladle.

Ellie flicked a hand at me – *'Drink?'* …

~

… Ellie mimed the drink gesture, but the strobes in the club made her actions disjointed, as if she were a puppet on a string. I didn't want a drink but nodded anyway. She disappeared into the throng.

I felt assaulted with heat and noise in the club. I shrank back, overwhelmed. The DJ in the booth thought he was in Ibiza with his glow-in-the-dark headset. The dance floor was taken up almost exclusively by girls and their friends; the young men congregated at the bar watching them. I blinked. Flashing lights were everywhere. Anything white glowed luminous: tee shirts, dresses, teeth.

I had to get out of there.

I staggered towards the toilets. The swing door felt cool to the touch in the warm air and as I passed the threshold, the din outside receded. Soundproof. It suddenly felt odd standing on the tiles, listening to hand dryers blaring and taps running as women and girls chatted at the mirrors as they repaired their make-up. Behind me, someone was retching in a stall.

'You all right, love?' A brassy woman with bright red lipstick that matched her handbag and shoes stopped next to me. She looked old, about my Mum's age. What was she doing here?

'I'm fine.' I said, even though I felt far from it.

The brassy woman shrugged and edged past me, giving me a wide berth for fear I throw up on her shoes. I caught sight of my reflection in the mirror. I looked drawn and pale with a greenish tinge. I went over to the sink and turned the tap on, washing my face, forgetting my make-up. I looked at myself: my mascara had run, my foundation in streaks. Great.

'There you are!'

Olivia appeared in the toilets next to me as if by magic. She carried a drink that was violet with an umbrella and several straws in it.

'You look like Hell.' She declared, slurping up her drink at the same time.

'I think I have a bug.' I said, my stomach growling in protest just at the sight of Olivia drinking.

'Yeah right.' Olivia smiled, 'You can't take your ale.'

My head was pounding. 'Vodka. I was drinking vodka.'

'Whatevs.' Olivia said brightly. She reached in her pocket, pulling out a lipstick and an eye pencil. 'Let's get you sorted out.'

Five minutes later and I looked like I had been punched in both eyes and had a fat lip. I was past caring. Back in the club, Olivia gave me a hug and said she'd fetch me a coke. She got swallowed up in the throng at the bar. I tried to find my way off the dance floor, but everywhere were couples kissing or dancing. Faces leered around me.

'Hey Jaz, you okay?' Niall seemed to materialise next to me, out of nowhere.

I could barely hear Niall's voice above the din of the music, but his face looked concerned. With horror, I realised I was leaning against him. He was actually holding me up! Yet try as I might, I could not get my feet to behave. I kept lurching against him like a ragdoll. So. Embarrassing.

Niall turned to a blonde guy in a blue and red Hawaiian shirt and said something like, *She's drunk, I gotta go.* His expression grim, Niall turned back to me and helped me out of the club.

Fresh, cold air hit me as we made our way out. Nausea welled up from my stomach. I broke away from Niall threw up, into a bin. The Doorman shouted after us, warning Niall not to come back in with me. Niall ignored him and sat me down on the curb. I took grateful, big gulps of air before realising what a sight I must look.

'Sorry.' I was mortified.

'S'all right.' Niall pressed a button on his phone, it went straight to voicemail. 'Ellie, I know you're in there. We're outside.'

He slid the phone back in his pocket.

'How much have you had to drink?' Niall said, 'Do you think you need to go to the hospital?'

'No … No!' I said, horrified. If Niall took me to the hospital, they would call Mum. And then a whole world of pain would ensue. 'I just had a bit too much, that's all. I'll be fine now, the club was doing my head in.'

Niall looked unsure.

'I feel better now …' *I've thrown up*, I almost said, stopping myself just in time before I embarrassed myself further. *Eeugh.*

'Okay.' Niall sighed.

The doors to the club opened up again and Ellie appeared, hands on her hips. 'Oh great. You realise we can't go back in now?' She admonished me. She rounded on Niall, next: 'Gotta save the world, haven't you?'

'Hardly,' Niall said dryly. 'She's your friend, you should have been looking after her.'

She's your friend. That stung. I was supposed to be Niall's girlfriend, wasn't I? I attempted to say the words, but that sour taste was back in my mouth … I was sure I was going to throw up again.

Behind me, Ellie and Niall continued to argue until a police car stopped beside the club. A young police officer got out of the car, leaving her much older partner inside. The young police officer looked nervous and had her notebook at the ready. Everything about her screamed, 'newbie'. The partner was watching her, so it had to be some sort of test. Brilliant.

'What's your name, love?' She said to me.

Ellie came running over to deflect the police officer. 'She's called Jasmine. She's fine. She's just had a dodgy kebab, that's all. We're taking her home.'

There was a pause as we all waited for the young police officer to digest this information. Her eyes darted from me, to Ellie, to Niall and then back to me again. The young police officer looked as if she'd rather be anywhere but here. That made two of us. Or four of us … Niall and Ellie were terrified as well.

'Okay.' The police officer said at last. We had to stop ourselves from sighing with relief. 'You take Jasmine straight home, you hear?'

We watched the police officer get back in the car and then ran/hobbled along The Strand, towards the multi-storey where Niall had left his car.

'I really thought she was going to bust us then.' Niall said.

'As if.' Ellie said, like it had never been in doubt and she *hadn't* had her heart in her mouth the whole time.

We all laughed, despite ourselves.

~

Back at the Grange, a there was a burst of hard rain against the windowpane. It sounded like someone had thrown gravel against the glass. A storm was brewing.

'Send everyone home.' Vic declared.

'No.' Ellie replied, resolute.

The two girls' eyes locked and for a moment, I was certain it was Ellie who was going to back down. Surely not? Some sort of power struggle was going on but I didn't know why, or what it was about. It must pre-date Ellie's time in Winby.

Abruptly, Victoria appeared to deflate. 'Fine.'

She stalked through to the other room, the weight of Ellie's triumph on her back.

'Everything okay?' I enquired.

'Yes. Why wouldn't it be?' Ellie said too quickly, her eyes shining. I'd never seen Ellie cry. Ellie was always in complete control, her outer shell seemingly impenetrable. But every now again I'd see a flash of … *something*. As if another Ellie was inside her, fighting to get out. But then she'd disappear again and the confident, capable Ellie would be back, as if she'd never gone away.

I took a sip of my punch. Wow. It was very, very strong.

'Very sophisticated.' Olivia drawled, 'What do you call it?'

'How Slut's Schnapps?' Ellie proffered a wide and seemingly innocent smile.

But Olivia only matched her grin, plucking another cherry from the bowl. 'Oh I dunno … I prefer Superiority Complex. Rolls off the tongue, don't you think?'

'Okay,' I said, eager to stop a blow out before it began. 'Let's take the punch through, shall we?'

Thirty-Seven

We carried the punch through, placing it on the coffee table. I clocked Becky Jarvis was on the other side of Niall, trying to get his attention. Even though Niall turned his body almost ninety degrees away from her, she wasn't taking the hint. I squeezed myself onto the sofa, next to him.

'Hi.' I kissed him full on the lips, in front of everyone.

I could see Becky Jarvis' face drop in the corner of my eye. Hah! I didn't even care when the others jeered and whistled. Vodka had made me brave, but it was about time.

Someone put Netflix on and fired up a horror movie. The punch was so strong, it soon got everyone talking. Andrew and Jake kept up a hilarious running commentary during the movie, on who would die next and how. Laughing, I noticed Jenny Keller was not watching, but staring at Nat Williams. He was not paying her the same attention. He stretched across two kitchen chairs, smoking a joint next to the open window with one of his crew. If Nat had seen Jenny giving him evils, he made out he didn't. What was Jenny's problem? Must be an Ex-girlfriend thing. I wondered if Andrew knew Jenny was still hung up on Nat.

Olivia appeared to be enjoying herself, chatting with people amiably. Vic appeared to be disgusted by her presence. She ignored my best friend, but that was handy. Vic did keep making eyeballs at Ellie, who appeared more and more defeated as the evening wore on.

The rain didn't stop. Through the big front glass windows of The Grange we could see the waves thrash up against the sea wall, some of the tide lapping up on to the patio. Nat closed the window and sat in the bay window alone. He was no longer watching the movie. He stared up at the moon peeking through the clouds, over the top of the headland. Jenny muttered something to Olivia and now they both stared over at him.

'Okay, what's going on?' I murmured to Olivia.

Olivia shrugged. 'Nothing. Why do you ask?'

There was something wooden, false about her voice. Before I could argue, Vic interrupted, appearing in front of the television. She was fully dressed now: a white vest top that actually fitted and a pencil cut denim skirt with rips and patches she'd probably paid extra for.

She held up an empty wine bottle, a drunken smirk on her face. 'Who's for spin the bottle?'

'Vic ...' Ellie began, but a sharp look from her friend silenced her. She sighed and sat back on the sofa.

Niall looked to me and shrugged: why not? There was a chorus of 'me' from the others, though Jenny muttered something to Andrew about wanting to go.

'C'mon, Jen.' Nat's eye was drawn to her at last.

But Jenny turned her entire body away from her Ex, pulling on the drunk and oblivious Andrew's arm. 'I want to go.'

'But the party's just getting started!'

Vic's gaze was on Olivia the whole time. Something in my gut tightened as Victoria said this: I felt sure the Spin

The Bottle game was a set-up of some kind. I didn't want to find out, I wanted to go home.

I got up and grabbed my bag, but Niall pulled me back onto the sofa, his face earnest. 'Don't go.'

'I'm tired, I'll see you tomorrow? Promise.' Niall looked disappointed, but fine with it. I turned back to my best friend, 'Let's go, Olivia.'

Olivia didn't budge. 'I'm up for a game.'

I looked at Olivia in surprise. She hated games like Spin The Bottle, she thought they were for middle school kids. In fact, she hadn't even played them when we were actually in middle school.

I looked at my best friend, then at Vic. Some sort of unspoken challenge had passed between them. This could get ugly. I tried to make her see sense.

'It's almost midnight.' I said. This was our code for getting out of something. If ever a party sucked or a night out was going South, we'd check the time and say this to the other.

But Olivia pretended she didn't know what I meant. 'Just one game.'

~

In Niall's car, sleep had settled over me for the duration of the ride home from Exmorton. The drive passed in what seemed like moments. Before I knew it, I was being shaken awake. I awoke, my head in a daze, outside The Grange, which was in darkness.

Something was wrong.

I sat up straight, dread hitting me. 'Where's Olivia!'

Niall rounded on Ellie. 'You had someone else with

you?'

Ellie rolled her eyes, still a little drunk. 'Just Olivia.'

She looked at me and Niall, seemingly unfazed.

'Oh come on! You know she'll be fine.'

I turned to Niall. 'We have to go back and get her.'

'I said we'd be back by now.' Niall looked at the clock. One o' clock.

'You're an adult, you don't have a curfew surely?' I replied, confused.

'Not a curfew, it's about 'consideration'. Apparently.' He massaged his brow as if he felt a headache coming on. 'If we come in at God knows when, you know Mum will kick off.'

'But … But … How is Olivia going to get home?' I was panic-struck. 'She won't have enough money for a taxi! I'll go and get her myself if I have to.'

It was false bravado. I had no idea how I would do that. I didn't drive and didn't have the money to get into Exmorton and back. Even if I woke up Mum, she didn't have a car and never kept that amount of cash in the house.

Niall sighed. 'Fine, I'll take you.'

It was not fine.

'Count me out.' Ellie got out the passenger side. 'You run around Exmorton looking for the local bike if you want, I'm going to bed.'

She slammed the door and went back inside The Grange.

Niall drove me back to Exmorton in silence. His knuckles gripping the steering wheel were white. I could tell he was annoyed with me.

'I'm sorry.' I said, breaking the silence at last.

He didn't answer.

I called Olivia's mobile for the fourteenth hundredth

time: straight to voicemail. She would be out of charge by now. *Hi, this is Olivia, leave a message, byeeeeeee... BEEP.* I hung up again.

We reached Exmorton just as all the clubs on The Strand finished for the night. Massive queues of club-goers lined up outside the kebab shop and curry house. Others gathered on the pavement and even in the road, forcing Niall to cruise at about two miles an hour as we tried in vain to spot Olivia. I wound down the window and peered out.

'Hey!'

My spirits lifted for a microsecond, until I saw who it was. Dressed in pink this time, wearing fairy wings and glitter on her face like a six-year-old, it was Jenny Keller. To my irritation, Niall stopped the car. Jenny came over, smiling like a loon as always. She was holding Andrew Franklin's hand.

'Hi Jenny.' I said dully, 'Seen Olivia?'

'No... Yeah!' Andrew interrupted, before the drunk Jenny could reply. He always spoke slowly, like stereotypical surf dudes off TV. 'Man, was she mad with you going off like that!'

'She's with you?' I was hopeful.

'No, she left ... She went to look for you.' Jenny almost fell over. Andrew held her up. '... Isn't she with you?'

'Can we, like, get a lift?' Andrew said.

'Sure.' Niall replied, exasperated. As Jake and Jenny clambered into the back seat, he turned to me, now in the passenger's seat. 'Now what?'

I grabbed my bag and pressed '2' on my phone, speed dialling Olivia's number. It went straight to voicemail again. Dread settled over me. I felt sick. Olivia could be anywhere! *And it was all my fault.*

It wasn't difficult to find the young police officer in the throng of under-age drinkers. She was taking notes next to the kebab shop, making half-hearted attempts to threaten teens into going home.

'You get your kebab and then go straight back, you hear?'

I recognised one of them: Moses Braunton. He had produced ID that said he was twenty-one. The young police officer couldn't be fooled. Moses looked about twelve. But if she took him back to the tank at Exmorton station, she'd have to take them all. Frankly, there were just too many to make that kind of stand. Her partner sat in the patrol car and ate a kebab from the same shop as the club-goers.

'Excuse me.' I said in a small voice.

The police officer turned on her heel and looked at me accusingly. Self-conscious, I blotted my hands on my skirt.

'My friend … I've lost my friend.' I said.

A couple of boys in the kebab line tittered at my choice of words. I was so worried about Olivia I just didn't care. The young police officer raised her eyes skywards as if she didn't have time for this nonsense. I gave her Olivia's age, address, phone number and description. I even managed to find a workable photo of her on my phone, which I texted to the police officer's.

Five minutes later and I was assured they'd 'do all they could' to find Olivia and make sure she was safe, not that that made me feel any better.

'What if something's happened to her?' I fretted in the car, on the way back to Winby with Niall. The other two had crashed out in the back.

'Guess you shouldn't have left her then.' Niall's gaze was set on the road. No question mark. He thought I was to blame. He wasn't wrong, either.

Niall dropped me off outside Olivia's house.

'I'm sorry,' I said again. I hated that Niall thought I was an idiot, almost as much as I hated the idea of leaving Olivia alone.

Niall's expression was grim. 'Let's just hope she's okay.'

He drove back towards the seafront, towards The Grange. What the hell would I say to Jim? *Hi, sorry, but I lost your daughter!* would hardly cut it. I gathered my resolve and rang the doorbell. There was movement inside the hall, a light came on and the front door opened.

'What the hell are you doing?' Olivia hissed. 'Dad's been on nights all week, he'll kill us if you wake him up!'

I blinked, hardly able to believe my eyes. Olivia was in her pyjamas, her make-up badly removed, black mascara marks around her eyes. But very much safe and well. Thank God!

'I'm so sorry, I didn't mean to …' I tried to fling my arms around her but was repelled.

'… Tell it to someone who cares.' Olivia slammed the door in my face.

~

That was why I'd brought Olivia tonight, to The Grange and Ellie's party. I wasn't going to let her down again.

Niall shook me awake again. 'All right, sleepyhead?'

I blinked my eyes to find a game of Spin The Bottle going on. I had dropped off for a minute or two. I must have been drunker than I thought.

He gave that lopsided grin. 'You playing, or what?'

'Go on then.' I shrugged.

Vic had reorganised everyone on the floor, moving the

boys around. I had dropped off. Ellie had thawed, though I noted Jenny Keller and Andrew had gone. Nat was still there, though. Across from him, Olivia stared at Vic, then called me over.

'Switch with me, Jaz.'

'Okay.' I didn't see why Olivia didn't want to sit near Nat, but it made no difference to me. Niall let go of my hand and took his place in the circle.

Vic smiled. 'Everyone ready?'

Thirty-Eight

After a few practice-runs, the bottle landed on Nat, its end pointing squarely at Jake Harrington. Both lads looked at each other, squeamish, their normal bravado vanished.

'I'll take a dare.' Nat said immediately.

'That's not the game.' Olivia had a smirk on her face. She knew Nat would not like the thought of kissing someone of the same gender. 'You're thinking of Truth or Dare.'

Nat shook his head. 'I don't care. I'm not kissing a bloke.'

Ellie rolled her eyes. 'Fine. The dare is … kiss Jake!'

We all laughed.

Nat's face flushed red. 'Come on, that's not fair!'

'It's the rules!' Olivia started clapping.

We all joined in, unable to resist. 'Nat, Nat, Jake, Jake …'

Jake shrugged. 'I don't doubt my masculinity.'

'Good for you.' Nat muttered.

'Come on already!' Vic declared, 'Let's get this over with!'

Jake grinned and puckered up, pointing to his lips. Nat scowled, then lunged forward and gave Andrew a peck on the cheek.

'Swizz!' Ellie was shrieking with laughter. Jake sat back down next to her and pushed her, she fell over started braying again.

The game started over. I was almost glad we stayed.

Until the bottle landed on Niall, the end pointing at Olivia.

'You made that happen.' Olivia pointed a finger at Vic.

'Of course I didn't.' Vic replied (she had).

A hush settled over the room. The others watched me and Olivia square up to each other. Did I really mind Niall kissing Olivia? There was a part of me that wanted to say 'no'. But that other, jealous side of me wondered if he might suddenly prefer her. Olivia was so much more experienced than me! Just like him. Maybe he'd prefer her?

Olivia sighed. 'Dare, then.'

'Oh, don't you start.' Vic commanded. 'You have to kiss him.'

I looked to Niall.

He rolled his eyes. 'Stop causing trouble, Vic.'

'As if I'd kiss him, anyway. He's my best friend's boyfriend.'

'None of this has to be a big deal. It's just a stupid game.' Niall announced, squeezing my hand with his. Relief descended over me.

Ellie, still drunk as hell, decided to settle the impasse. She grabbed the bottle. 'Spin again!'

The bottle span round and round. But Olivia was popular with fate, because this time the neck ended up pointing at her. Olivia paled. At the other end …

… Nat Williams.

'Well, well.' Nat flashed Olivia a wolfish grin. 'Not like the first time though, hey Olivia?'

The atmosphere at the party did a complete three sixty. It had been awkward when Vic wanted Olivia and Niall to kiss, but this was something else. I knew Nat was referencing when he and Olivia had slept together at Sam West's party. Back then, Nat had been going out with Jenny Keller. Everyone had talked about for weeks. Jenny's stricken face earlier swam back into my mind. But she and Olivia had moved on since then. What was I missing?

'Oh, there wasn't much kissing as I remember.' Olivia said through gritted teeth.

Nat winked. 'No. Nor me, actually. Little demon, you were.'

'You're disgusting.' Olivia snarled.

Nat held out both hands in surrender. 'Hey. It's not my fault if you got buyer's regret …!'

Olivia scrambled to her feet. Within seconds she was out the living room and towards the kitchen. I heard the horrendous weather outside as she opened the front door. It slammed after her.

I let go of Niall's hand and looked for my bag, the sandals I'd kicked off earlier in the night. 'I have to go after her.'

'Oh, let her go,' Victoria said. 'If she's going to get in a strop …'

'Be quiet, Vic!' Ellie erupted like a geyser.

Vic looked at her friend with bugged eyes. Ellie had clearly never uttered those words to Victoria in her life.

I finally located my sandal. I didn't have time for Ellie and Vic right now. I didn't know what was happening, but it was far from okay. Behind me, Niall landed both hands on Nat's lapels. He wrenched him to his feet. They were fairly evenly matched, though Nat played football. He could take

Niall if he wanted.

But Nat just laughed at him. 'You a white knight, or something?'

'I don't know what's gone on but get the hell out.' Niall growled.

I loved him for that.

I ran out, after Olivia.

Thirty-Nine

Only wearing sandals, my feet were soaked and cold within moments of leaving The Grange. The rest of me was too; I'd only brought a light jacket. A million thoughts rushed through my brain as I raced after Olivia. The tide was going out now and with it, the foul weather.

Winby's flood defences had been tested. One of the red lights on the system was flashing. A man in sou'wester and huge anorak was shining a torch along the wall, checking for leaks. I noted Flossie's and The Moon pub had their sandbags out. So did the arcade and ironmonger's on the seafront. Raging rivulets of water made it down the high street, towards the cove and the beach beyond, bubbling ferociously at the curb-side beside the pavement.

I was surprised not to see Olivia. She'd only just left. Shivering, I pulled up my jacket collar and placed my hands under my armpits in an ineffectual attempt to keep warm. The clock tower sounded its tinny half hour chime. Eleven thirty. It only took seven minutes to walk to my house from The Grange; five from the seafront to Olivia's. I must have just missed her as she turned the corner off the high street, up ahead.

Jim's car was missing as usual from the driveway as I

drew level with Olivia's house. Anxious, I peered through the window into the sitting room. Jim was not in there. None of the lights were on. I checked for the key in the usual place: it was gone. I made my way down the side of the house, in darkness. Olivia's bedroom was dark too. My hand strayed to my phone in my pocket. I wondered if I should call the police, say Olivia had run off into the night. But Jim WAS the police. I hovered, indecisive.

'She make it back okay? Is she in?'

The voice made me jump. I turned to find an equally drenched Nat Williams a few feet behind me. One of his nostrils was bloody. A dull satisfaction bloomed in my belly. So, Niall had hit him, then. I imagined my boyfriend back at The Grange, running his knuckles under a cold tap. He was not a natural fighter. Maybe Ellie would bandage his hand for him.

'What do you care?' I glowered at him. 'Jerk.'

Everyone always said Nat Williams was such a good guy. But there was something dark about him. The arrogant swagger of a guy who could have whatever he wanted. That was why I was surprised Olivia had gone anywhere near him at that party. She'd always said she couldn't stand him.

Nat cocked his head at me, that way he always did. 'Frigid little bitch, aren't you?'

'What?'

The about-turn in the conversation wrongfooted me. Even though Nat *was* a jerk, I expected him to at least try and defend himself. He moved forwards, his broad body blocking my way out. I was pinioned between the side wall of Olivia's house and the tall fence into the next door's garden.

'I said … Frigid … Little … Bitch.' He had wide smile

on his face as he said those hateful words.

I froze. My brain refused to catch up with my body, which was on red alert. It felt like I was watching from above as Nat advanced on me, his pale white skin glowing in the moonlight. Too late, all the jigsaws pieces fitted together.

Nat had done this before and got away with it.

To Jenny Keller.

To Olivia.

They'd never slept with him, he had taken what he wanted.

That was why they hated him.

That was why they didn't hate each other.

Olivia had kept it a secret, all this time.

Nat reached forward and grabbed me, slamming me against the wall. My head hit Olivia's bedroom windowsill. Stars sprang up in front of my eyes. Still I couldn't move.

I'm sorry, Olivia.

Too late, I knew why she'd never told me after Sam West's party last year. I'd assumed she'd split Jenny and Nat up, just like everyone else.

'Think you're so much better than everyone, don't you?' Nat clamped a hand over my mouth. 'And that posh boyfriend of yours.'

Inside, I was screaming. His hand was over my nose as well. I struggled to breathe. Would he smother me? Would he kill me, right here, outside my best friend's house? I felt his cold hand move up under my skirt, grope between my legs.

Then I felt, rather than heard a hard *thwack*. Nat reeled, his head wavering on his neck, his grip on me loosening. My nose free at last, I gasped in the night air.

A second *whack* came next, across Nat's shoulders. He dropped to his knees, crying out in pain.

I looked up, stupefied, unable to understand what had just happened.

Olivia stood over Nat, a hockey stick in hand.

Still on his knees, Nat shot daggers at Olivia. 'You're gonna regret that.'

'I don't think so.' Olivia did not look triumphant. She looked vacant.

Behind her, the guy in the sou'wester from the seafront appeared, shining his big torch on us. As he drew nearer, I saw it was one of the lifeboatmen, Alec, my Granfer's mate. His lined face was drawn with concern. He was a huge man, bigger than Nat. As soon as Nat saw him, all the fight left him. He was a coward.

It was over.

Forty

'Where is she?'

Mum rushed into Olivia's front room. She looked wild with panic, like a cornered animal. I sat, shivering on Olivia's old, stained couch. My best friend had her arm around me. Later she'd tell me she had been at home, she just hadn't turned the light on in her room. When Nat had slammed me against the wall of the house, the force had rattled the windowpane. She'd grabbed her hockey stick and run, beckoning for Alec as he walked down the road from the seafront.

'Darling, I'm so sorry. Thank God you're okay.' Olivia moved aside and Mum enveloped me in her arms. She smelled of white musk from The Body Shop and childhood.

I let my head drop on to her shoulder. I was so cold, but it had nothing to do with my wet clothes. Everyone said Nat Williams was a good bloke. Sure, he was arrogant and loved himself, but to do *that* … And not just to me, either. As the thought sprouted in my brain, I looked up at my best friend.

'I'm s-s-sorry.' The words escaped through my chattering teeth. 'I never even asked about Sam West's party …'

Olivia shook her head. 'I never told you, Jaz. You're not a mind reader.'

'B-B-But I just assumed …' I closed my eyelids. They

felt so heavy.

'Well, it was true.' Olivia's gaze was far away. She was back at Sam West's party. 'I did know he was going out with Jenny, but I'd been drinking and didn't care. Until I felt guilty and wanted to stop.'

The horror of what my best friend *wasn't* saying prickled through me. So that was why Olivia and Jenny had been muttering in corners all summer. They'd been supporting each other, dealing with all of this on their own.

'Why didn't you and Jenny go to the police?'

'Jenny begged me not to. It was worse for her, it hadn't just been once.'

'Once is enough.' I shuddered. 'There's no scale to this, Olivia.'

Olivia shrugged. '*We* decided it was better if she broke up with Nat and let everyone assume what had happened. Besides, who would have believed me? I went upstairs willingly with Nat at Sam's. Everyone saw me.'

'It wasn't your fault.'

Olivia smiled, but it didn't reach her eyes. 'Can't rape a slut.'

'No. Don't say that. Not about yourself.' Mum reached out her other arm.

Olivia hesitated, then pulled in closer, so Mum was hugging both of us.

Jim arrived home next, still in uniform. He told us Alec had met one of his colleagues outside with Nat. The lifeboatmen had watched over him for forty minutes in his car. I was still surprised Nat had capitulated so easily, but where could he go? Winby was small and there had been too many witnesses. Nat would have to rely on Daddy buying him an expensive lawyer to get out of this one.

Not a flicker of emotion passed across Jim's face as Olivia told him what had happened outside their home. I wondered if he would start taking down details in his little policeman's notebook, but he didn't. Mum kept rubbing my arm, reminding me she was there. I could hear her grinding her teeth in anger.

'The others from the station are on their way.' Jim's voice was grave.

'No! No! You can't! I can't face it!'

Even as objected, I knew it was fruitless. It was done. I realised why Olivia hadn't told me: shame washed over me, followed by helplessness. I stopped, defeated. Did I really have any choice in this?

Jim leant down, looking into my eyes. 'Olivia's told me everything. There's already been one more, this Jenny Keller. And that's just who we know about. Maybe there's more. Do you want it to happen to anyone else?'

'Don't ever put that on her.' Mum's voice was cold.

Jim sighed. 'I didn't mean it like that.'

'They'll say it's my fault.' The words burst out of my lips before I thought them through. I hated the thought of the others from college knowing.

'It'll be hard, sweetheart. I won't lie to you about that.' Mum took a shaky breath, 'But it's time that boy got what he deserves.'

Olivia put her hand in mine. 'We'll support you. Me and Jenny. We'll do this together?'

I looked at Mum, then my best friend's earnest face. She had been so brave. Olivia had let everyone think she was the bad guy, just to get Jenny out of that terrible situation with Nat. Jenny no doubt had the scars, but she had Andrew now. Who had Olivia had in her corner? She had crashed from one bad situation to the next one, thanks to me sucking up to Ellie. I was the worst.

Well, I could stand up now and do what was right, even if it was difficult. I owed it to Olivia and Jenny. But I also owed it to myself.

I curled my hand round hers. 'Together.'

Forty-One

Still the middle of the night, Jim's colleagues from Exmorton descended on the house. It felt surreal, watching people in-all-one suits comb through Olivia's front garden and the side alley, just like on TV. Jim stood on the sidelines, watching, but unable to help. 'Conflict of interest' one officer said, a young woman with a dark bob and a large mole above her lip.

I was checked over by a paramedic. An ambulance stood idle in the driveway, its blue light rolling around, no siren. I told them I didn't want to go to the hospital. Interrupted by Olivia, Nat hadn't left any marks on me. They went to Alec's car and checked Nat over, as the police insisted before taking him to the station.

Mum didn't want me or Olivia to follow them to the lane, but I insisted. We linked arms and watched him, head hung low, as they told him to lift his shirt. They said he was fine, just nasty bruising.

'Good.' Olivia said, loud enough for him to hear.

He wouldn't look us in the eye. Coward.

As dawn appeared over the horizon, I finally left Olivia's, with a card to attend the police station in the afternoon to make a statement. Olivia told me she would come by the next day. I hugged her before I left, reiterating it was not hers or Jenny's fault. But Olivia just nodded, averting her gaze, as if she thought otherwise, or that I was just saying it. I hated Nat for making her think that about herself.

Mum and I found Niall, slumped asleep on our doorstep. When we woke him and fed him some hot chocolate, he said he'd come up to Olivia's, but been turned away at the police cordon. He'd been panicking all night. I checked my phone and sure enough, there were about twenty missed calls and double that of text messages. I told him what had happened. He blamed himself, for letting Nat go. But it wasn't his fault either. Only Nat's.

Still agitated, I was unable to sleep. Anger had replaced my shock now. I could feel the adrenaline surge through my body. Mum didn't want me to go out but relented when Niall said he would go with me. We left the flat again and marvelled at how normal everything seemed. People were going to work, opening shutters on the seafront, filling the penny falls in the arcade with oversized cups of coins. Unlike the previous day, the sky was bright blue, the sun shining.

The deluge of rain had left its mark. The businesses along the seafront, including the fish and chip shop and The Moon were a foot deep in floodwater. The tide had breached the wall of sandbags the lifeboat men had lined the sea wall with. A single neon yellow bucket floated off, down the road.

The Grange rose out of the murky water, its patio disappeared, though the house was dry. We could see Ellie at the patio window, staring down at me. She gestured at me and Niall to stay where we were.

Moments later, she appeared down the back steps of

the grand house, pulling on a cardigan as she went. 'Police came here this morning?'

I let Niall explain, this time. I was suddenly too tired to manage it. I sat down on the sea wall, exhausted. I would be asleep soon, right here if I didn't get back.

'And to think … Nat Williams was in *my* house.' Ellie said, ever the drama queen.

'It's not always about you!' I snapped.

'No. No of course not.' Ellie sighed. 'As long as you're okay. Will you tell Olivia … I hope she's okay, too? I mean it.' She added, realising I might think she was being sarcastic.

'You've got her number. Tell her yourself.' I said in a clipped voice.

That afternoon, Mum escorted me to little Winby police station where I made my statement. Shame burning in my cheeks, I made sure I left nothing out. I wanted to be certain of giving the police their best shot at charging Nat. I didn't deserve his treatment and I had failed Olivia enough. I listed every single person at Ellie's house the night before, as many addresses as I knew. I also told them what I had heard at college, about Sam's West's Party, as well as about Jenny Keller and how I was kicking myself.

'It's always easier with hindsight.' Mum said later, seated across the table from me in Teddy's.

The bell over the door drew my attention. There was Jenny Keller, looking uncharacteristically cheer-less, dressed in black. On either side of her, her Mum and Step-Dad. They held Jenny between them as if they were some kind of forcefield. They looked like good parents, why hadn't she told them? I felt anger well up from deep inside of me. Didn't she know that if she'd said something back then, before anything had happened to Olivia, all this could have been avoided?!

But then I laughed inwardly at my own hypocrisy. It was too easy for me to call Jenny out. I didn't know every detail of Jenny Keller's life or problems. I did wish Jenny and Olivia hadn't lied by omission over that had happened at Sam West's party, but then I had no business telling others what they should have done. They had their reasons. There was only one person to blame for this situation and it wasn't me, Jenny or Olivia.

I attempted to smile at Jenny, who came straight over to my table.

'I'm so sorry.' Jenny's pale face was earnest.

I shook my head. 'This was down to Nat, no one else.'

We hugged, before Jenny re-joined her parents at one of the tables by the window.

'I'm proud of you, you know.' Mum said. 'And things don't stay the same, remember. I know it's bad now, but things will change. They have to, it's impossible for time to stand still. It has to move on.'

I digested Mum's words. Once they would have filled me with despair. I would have seen only the negative in change, but now I realised it was neither bad, nor good. Just life.

I smiled. 'Thanks Mum …'

Epilogue

Saturday, August 25th

… And with those words, came that sense of time juddering to a standstill, before speeding up. I couldn't catch my breath. I saw various images flash past me, on fast-forward, like moments through a train carriage window:

Olivia, in bed, eating a large packet of bacon crisps …
Jenny Keller, waving with that cheery grin …
Niall, attempting to kiss me but me jerking away from him
…
Ellie, standing in her kitchen in her pyjamas, buttering toast, telling me Olivia couldn't come to the party that evening.

Olivia sat across the table from me, now. 'You okay?'
How long is forever … Sometimes just one second.
I wasn't sure why those words returned to me again. Next, I saw Kevin seated at the bottom of my bed, saying The White Rabbit's words again in his flawless Scottish accent. Though I had forced myself not to think of him for a long time, suddenly grief flooded through me. I had never

asked for Kevin to become part of my life, but I had never asked for him to be taken away from me, either. I knew that it was between him and Mum, but I had loved him too. I decide to look him up and drop him a line on Facebook when I get home. Most old people were on there.

'Yes, of course.' I tamped down my confusion. There was something familiar about the situation. Like I had traced these steps before: *déjà vu*. That's all it was.

How long is forever ...

As Olivia continued chatting, I thought back to the first time I had set eyes on Olivia. That seemed like forever ago ... But it also seemed like one second. That first day of nursery. The *thwack* of Olivia's skipping rope handles against my head, the salty taste of my own tears as I cried.

But most of all, the feel of Olivia's chubby arms around my neck, her own cries of apology, her promises she would never hurt me again. Olivia had stayed true to her word, all these years. Yes, sometimes Olivia could be demanding, petulant, even downright infuriating, but I always knew she was in my corner. She had been there for me my whole life. Olivia knew all my fears, hopes and dreams. She knew all my secrets and everything that had happened to me. She knew my weaknesses better than I did ... But she did not hold them against me.

I could not let her down. It was as simple as that.

In Teddy's, I looked again at my phone, Ellie's message: *YOU TELL HER OR I WILL*. I looked across the table at Olivia, who was now scrolling through her own screen. I tapped out a quick message and pressed send before I could change my mind.

I'M NOT COMING.

The bell rang over the shop door. Niall meandered in,

hands in his pockets.

'Hey.' I stood up and gave him a peck on the lips.

'Hey.' Niall looked surprised I had initiated it for once. 'You going to Ellie's thing tonight?'

I shake my head. 'Got training in the morning.'

'Oh thank God.' Niall breathed a sigh of relief, 'Maybe I'll go into Exmorton or something. I don't think I can stand hanging around with a million strangers Ellie has invited from Instagram!'

I laughed. Through the café window, Mum appeared outside Flossie's. She pretended to rearrange neon displays, but she was blatantly spying on us. We both gave her sarcastic little waves, smiles on our faces.

'Your Mum is so obvious.'

'Parents are always so embarrassing.'

Niall looked me up and down. I was still in my running clothes. 'How about another run?'

'Race more like.' I grinned, then indicated I was with Olivia. 'Can't right now.'

Niall nodded. 'How about I come to training in the morning, then?'

'It's early.' I warned.

'That's fine. I want to support you. See you then.' Niall kissed me on the lips again, then turned to make his order at the counter.

I sat back down with Olivia. I followed her glance across the café. By the mural, Jenny Keller sat with her boyfriend Andrew Franklin. I sensed something pass between her and Olivia, but I wasn't sure what. In fact, now I thought about it, Jenny had been orbiting around us for a while. Since Sam West's party, at least.

'Everything okay with you?' I asked.

Olivia's face froze with a plastic smile. ''Course.'

Now I was certain something was suss. 'Since when have you and Jenny Keller been friends?'

'Who said we're friends?' There was a wild look on Olivia's face.

I paused, choosing my words carefully. 'No one. It's just I keep seeing you and her. That's all … Okay, let me rephrase. Are *we* okay?'

I braced for impact.

Olivia's brow furrowed. She tossed her phone down. 'Kinda. Though to be honest, you've been a bit of a bitch this summer. Sucking up to Ellie, never standing up for me. What gives?'

I sighed. 'You're right. I've been an idiot.'

'Oh.' Olivia seemed to deflate. She had been expecting me to argue the toss.

I leaned forward, grabbing her hand. 'I haven't been there for you, before even this summer. I let college work take over. I'm sorry.'

Olivia didn't pull her hand away. But she couldn't look me in the eye, either. She touched the heel of one hand to her eye. I recognised the gesture straight away: I'd seen her do it a thousand times. She was trying not to cry. This was serious.

I touched foreheads with my best friend. 'What is it? You can tell me.'

I thought Olivia would shrug, give me another false grin. She didn't.

'Not here.' She muttered.

'We can go back to yours?' I offer.

Oliva nodded, her hand still in mine, her gaze cast on the floor. I grabbed my phone as we stood up. Before I put the phone back in my pocket, I noticed another notification from Ellie:

WHAT IF I SAID OLIVIA COULD COME?

But none of that mattered, now. So what if Ellie was having a party? I did not wish her ill – she was Niall's sister, after all – but I saw now that Ellie didn't want was best for me. She'd seen me as a project, someone to hang around with while she was stuck in Winby for the summer. I was lucky: a friend like Olivia was worth a hundred Ellies. Olivia had always been there for me.

Now it was my turn now to be there for her. I needed to find out what had been bothering her since Sam West's party. Whatever it was, we would face it as best friends.

I tap out a quick message: *NO THANKS. SEE YOU AROUND.*

Olivia stopped by the doorway of Teddy's to wait for me. I slipped my phone in my pocket and linked arms with my best friend.

The bell over the door rang as we left together.

The Intersection Series

by Lucy V Hay

On the eve of her eighteenth birthday, Lizzie finds herself pregnant: she's literally days away from her exam results and university beckons around the corner. The bright Lizzie has big plans, but can she have the life she wanted, with a baby in tow? What will her family and friends say? And what will the baby's father choose to do: stay out of it, or stand by her?

Proof Positive is powerful, pro-choice YA that is perfect for fans of John Green, Judy Blume and Sarah Dessen.

CPSIA information can be obtained
at www.ICGtesting.com
Printed in the USA
LVHW010110090121
676100LV00002B/309

9 781999 350116